Spirit Horse II

Carousel Horse Workbook
and Screenplay

Elizabeth Wiley MA JD, Pomo Elder

Order this book online at www.trafford.com
or email orders@trafford.com

Most Trafford titles are also available at major online book retailers.

Print information available on the last page.

ISBN: 978-1-4907-9240-8 (sc)
ISBN: 978-1-4907-9243-9 (e)

Trafford rev. 11/30/2018

 www.trafford.com
North America & international
toll-free: 1 888 232 4444 (USA & Canada)
fax: 812 355 4082

Dedicated to our horses, volunteers, and daily heroes who help each other whether high risk youth, first responders, veterans and their family members.

A HUGE SPECIAL THANK YOU to Blue Pearl Project for keeping our horses while we were recovering from cancer and accidents, and our stable burnt in a forest fire.

Donations may be made to their sanctuary at Blue Pearl Project@gmail.com. Or at their web site, Blue Pearl Project. com Even $5 makes a difference for a horse being rescued. Please mention Spirit Horse II and National Homes for Heroes when you donate. This is a veteran owned sanctuary, they have kept our horses working in therapy programs while we were recovering and getting ready to go back to our work.

Another HUGE special thank you to our Director, who got to be the director by being in the restroom when we got to the line on our 501 c 3 application which asked who the Director was. Our board looked around the room, and since she was not in the room, said PAT. Patricia McLaughlin has put so much of her experience, and expertise into the programs for high risk youth and children and teens with veteran family members and also her adult education credential work into helping both first responders and veterans find new careers after being injured on their jobs and no longer able to do the work they love. Congratulations to Pat for her nomination to those considered for the First Annual Southern California Social Justice servants of the people.

Introduction

This book is our training manual and workbook for those who want to start up, or increase services in equine therapy programs.

The original Carousel Horse is a children's book an inclusion book for teaching young people who may or may not be able to attend on site equine therapy. We have found using a screenplay allows young people to integrate the material even though they are not able to attend an on site program.

We do suggest K-9 programs where possible, many lock downs and youth probation programs while not able to allow the youth outside their facilities, do allow K-9 therapy teams INTO their facilities. We have had facilities through probation that have allowed us to trailer in a horse as well from time to time.

This book is also hopefully an inspiration to veterans, first responders, social workers, and others who would like to volunteer and grow animal assisted programs, or to start their own programs. Many veterans are finding small working farms to allow them to have a quiet career where families and school or community groups can come and learn about animals and farming. This is a splendid way to allow service to the community that they love, without the stress of police, fire, or military combat work.

Equine therapy has been utilized for small children with Down's Syndrome, or Cerebral Palsy, or other physical disabilities that have been show in research by Horses and Humans Research Foundation to have lasting positive results in mental, physical and emotional health of the riders.

When asked to create a program for foster children, Spirit Horse was created as a special crew of Boy Scouts of America. A judge asked if we could create a mandatory program for then Desert Storm veterans, who due to PTSD had had their children removed and often could not see them except for with a Court ordered liaison. Both men and women veterans had serious problems with their children being removed. This project worked with volunteer Veteran therapists, and paramedics who had worked in combat areas as well as the veterans and their children to create programs that worked.

We respect and admire all equine therapy programs, but there are some much more able than we to deal with more serious levels of PTSD, and we salute them and refer to them when needed. There are other animal assisted programs for veterans that are working. We NEED to remind those working with violent teens, violent criminals, and violent PTSD veterans that what works for a disabled child is NOT proper therapy for a mentally and emotionally effected adult. Especially for veterans, and teen and adult violent criminals, in Court mandated programs, there are special programs, do NOT attempt to deal with situations you are NOT equipped to deal with. There are some real horse and cattle ranches, owned and operated by veterans, or having programs assisted by veterans, and high risk youth that are VERY successful, we are completely aware that they are better equipped than we are to deal with those situations. Especially for combat, and special ops, and first responders who deal with violent and often deadly incidents, the best healing we suggest is a program that has others like themselves, as leadership in the programs. Some of the programs are live on site cattle ranches, or horse training sites that have their own therapists and alumni to help those who come after them.

WE, our therapists, psychiatrists and horse trainers, believe that those injured in critical and violent work such as military active duty, and first responders deserve to be helped heal, not be labeled as mentally ill and given expensive medications which they often describe to us as making them into zombies. New programs and research are also showing a significant number of both veterans and first responders with real neurological damage, NOT PTSD. We ask all of our riders to talk to a neurologist and get proper evaluation. One of the high risk youth in a lock down for violent offenders was found to have an operable brain tumor that had been causing his violent outbursts, certainly a better alternative to the spending of the rest of his life medicated in a mental hospital for violent adults. Another "mental" patients was a nurse, who "went beserk" one day. She too was locked up after a 72 hour hold. A new Director came into the county facility and had every single person there re-evaluated. He had her see a neurologist, she too had an operable brain tumor, and today is back to nursing and raising her daughter.

One of the young veterans suffered for many years, and when the new re-assess every veteran project was started, the doctors asked him why he had not told him is neck was broken when his tank was hit by a missile in Bosnia. He said to the doctor, in a dry voice, because the doctors took a quick look at me, and said, you are fine, and sent me to be a Hummer gunner in Iraq for a year, until I was hit by a roadside device and injured so badly they had to send me home. The doctors never noticed my neck I guess.

BUT they had listed his pain and short temper as PTSD, given him medications and a label, and lost him his chance to go to the Coast Guard and continue his medical education and become a Coast Guard medic and then doctor for Native American Veterans. Veterans listed as PTSD have most career doors shut to them.

Carousel Horse

Keiya lives in a room with horses. Looking around, she sees carousel horses, alone on stands, in carousels, on jewelry boxes, in music boxes, on posters, in photographs. Even smiling photographs of herself on a carousel horse merry-go-round with her Dad hugging her to keep her from falling.

Dad. Dad is so much fun, but since Keiya was injured in a car accident, he has to work two jobs to pay the medical and therapy bills, and she does not see him very often anymore. Keiya can hear Mom banging around in the kitchen. Mom never does anything quietly, even while mopping, or sweeping Mom turns on rock music, LOUD, and dances while she cleans the house. Mom is out there bashing the dishes and pans in, or out, of the dishwasher from the sounds.

Keiya is watching television. She loves to watch the horse channel. The show is changing. A young man is helped from his wheelchair on to a big horse, he rides into the show arena, and does a routine. Keiya is excited. He is riding alone. She listens to the announcer who is talking about the riding programs for the disabled.

Mom is closing the dishwasher, quiet for the moment, except for the click of the catch on the door. All of a sudden a horrible scream surrounds her, the house is shaking with the scream. "MOM". Mom rushes to Keiya. She cannot believe her eyes. Keiya is sitting forward in her wheelchair, excited and staring, pointing at the television. Mom sees a young child being led on a horse. A wheelchair is sitting behind in the corral. There are several people who walk beside the horse and are helping the young child on the horse.

Mom stops shaking, and Keiya starts talking excitedly. "Can I go too". Mom says, find more about it. Keiya moves to her desk, where her computer is. She keys in disabled riding programs for children and up comes a long list. Keiya and Mom begin to go over the programs in the list. They key in their own area, and find one that is not too far away.

Mom is not too sure, but Keiya is certain. "Can we go today?"

Mom says maybe not, because they have to call and ask. Mom calls, and Keiya screams again with joy when the stable manager says they CAN come today, classes go on six days a week, and they can come and find out about the programs.

While Mom is getting ready, Keiya sits restlessly in her chair. She absentmindedly turns on one of the carousel music boxes. Sitting and watching the tiny horses, manes covered with ribbons and flowers prancing around the small merry-go-round, Keiya imagines…..

She sees herself, on a horse, with mane and tail filled with flowers and ribbons. She and the horse are going round and round. Mom is surprised to find Keiya with a huge smile on her quiet, far away face when she comes to change her to her electric wheelchair to go into the van.

Mom and Keiya are driving in the van, the freeway is crowded and slow. Mom has her music up, LOUD, as usual. Keiya reaches across and turns it down. "Mom"

Mom looks at her for a brief second while driving. "Do you think I will really be able to ride a horse?"

Mom sighs, and says they will see what the stable manager has to say, and turns the music back up. Keiya looks out the window eagerly watching for the exit. The van goes up the exit and turns on to a two-lane road that leads out into the country. They are no longer in the city as they exit the freeway. Keiya sees houses with stalls and small corrals in front. Best of all, she sees horses, horses, horses as the van smoothly and LOUDLY, due to Mom's music, goes along towards the ranch.

Keiya sees the sign. It has a picture of a child riding a horse on the board. Mom turns into the driveway after being treated to another of Keiyas ear shattering screams. "This is it!" Keiya and Mom park and look around. They are surrounded by pathways for wheelchairs that lead to round corrals, they can see a large arena with many children riding in it. Each of the horses is being led by someone, and there is a person on each side of the horse.

Keiya and Mom cannot believe their eyes. The children, almost at the same moment, bend forward, and begin to kneel on their horse. The people next to them help them balance as needed. The children begin to do arm exercises. Over the head, on the shoulders, hands on knees, arms outstretched to the sides. Some of the riders are held on each side by the person walking next to the horse. The person leading the horse just continues to walk, quietly with the horse. Keiya moves her electric wheelchair over to the fence to peer through the bars to see them all better.

One by one, the children rise up on their feet. A few of the people walking next to a rider, jump up on the horse and hold the rider upright. The children begin the arm exercises again.

Some of them bend and touch their toes, all while the horse is walking on and on. The children slide down and sit, and pat the horses as they all stop. Each member of the group goes to a wheelchair and the children dismount and get settled into their chairs. Parents come into the arena to help them maneuver through the sand. A couple with electric wheelchairs with inflated tires like Keiya's just move on out by themselves through the open gate. The horse handlers then lead the horses out and to the barns, or towards another corral for a new class.

A woman wearing a sport shirt with the same logo as they saw on the sign in front of the ranch approaches Mom and Keiya. A large dog, who had been lying quietly outside the corral rises and comes over to Keiya and Mom at the same time. Keiya is so excited. Mom and Dad have never let her have a dog, they were afraid it might knock her chair down and hurt her. While Mom and the woman are talking, Keiya enjoys the closeness and smell of the dog who has come up and is looking her straight in the face. Because of the wheelchair, Keiya is almost at eye level of the dog.

Mom says that the lady is named Amber, and she is going to show Mom around, and go over the paperwork and rules. Keiya is going to go with one of the volunteers, and the dog, named Big Macs, the woman smiles and says it is because he is so big, but yes, he does love the hamburgers as well. A teenage girl, maybe a couple of years older than Keiya approaches and waits to be introduced. Amber tells Mom and Keiya that Bella has been a student at the stable since she was five, and now is a volunteer. Amber says she will let Bella tell her own story as she shows Keiya the ranch.

The two girls, and the dog head down one of the paths. Mom and Amber head for the stable office. Mom looks back, a little tense, Amber pats her on the arm, and leads her off with a smile. Keiya thinks Amber has a lot of experience with scared parents.

Bella tells Keiya that she is a foster child. That she used to be in a group home, her parents could no longer take care of her, so she had been placed in a group home until they could find the right foster home for her. The group home had brought all the children in the home to therapeutic riding lessons. Even after being placed in a foster home, Bella had continued to come to the ranch, and finally had started to volunteer to help other foster children make the adjustments in their lives. The two girls have reached the barns. A line of curious horse faces has popped out, a few whinnies and rumbles can be heard. Keiya is a little afraid of the huge animals, now that she is really right near them. Bella laughs and tells Keiya they are just begging for carrots. She shows her where the big bag of carrots is and that one is in the feed room of each of the barns, so the riders can give them to the horses. Bella takes a handful of carrots, and hands a lapful to Keiya. The two girls go down the row handing out carrots as Bella tells Keiya about each of the horses.

Most of the horses, explains Bella, belong to private owners. Some are rich and loan their horses to the program, Amber owns the stable and lets them keep them there free with the understanding that should something happen and money is a problem, Amber will let them know and they will begin to pay for the hay for their horses. The owners come and ride their own horses for the same use they had before they loaned them to the program. Each horse has a small calendar taped to the edge of the small tack box beside the stall door. Bella tells Keiya that this is the schedule for the horse so owners and the program know if the horse if free from classes or needs to go somewhere with the owner each day.

Some of the owners are old, or disabled, or have lost money due to losing their jobs, they loan their horses to the stable, with the understanding that should something happen, they will have to pay for hay themselves. Many of the owners volunteer in many ways in the programs. Some teach English, Math, Science in outdoors hands on classes for students who need them. Some teach about business and how to open and take care of bank accounts, and save for big purchases, such as tuition, cars, homes, and businesses in the future. Many have a special skill. Bella laughs as she tells Keiya about some of the delicious specialties volunteers teach all the students, volunteers and parents to make on cooking days.

A few of the horses belong to Amber. Some she bought, some were given to her by her sons when she herself was disabled and they wanted to cheer her up. No one knew that gift would lead to her starting a whole new career, and helping others start up broken lives.

Many of the horses, either owned by others, or by Amber are injured, or old, or too harmed by people to be in the program full time. One horse is 39 years old. Once he was a race horse, then spent many years out to stud, when he got tumors that prevented live foal birth count being high, he was sold at auction. The buyer could not handle him, and sold him again at auction to a man who wanted him for a parade horse, but could never get him to calm down enough. He was sold to another man who had him gelded before his girlfriend started to train him, he almost killed her running away in a mountain area. He was going to the auction again when Amber bought him because he had been next to her horse for more than a year, and she felt bad knowing he would probably get sold down and down and beaten into submission or killed for not behaving. She and a disabled retired rider took three years to retrain him, and now he had worked with children for more than 25 years. He still loved to be groomed, washed, and sometimes, with little children ridden for the program. Amber told Keiya how the two women, one in the saddle, and one on the ground, used reins, and two sets of lines to make sure he behaved until finally he just gave in and behaved. They had called the style of training "Upsy/downsy" because one rider was up, and one was on the ground to control the horse without violence until he got the training he needed to be safe. Amber said it had worked well because when Amber got cancer and in a car accident and could no longer ride, she had continued to train with older riders, and volunteers using the same "Upsy/downsy" method.

He had a little pail of special treats hanging near his stall door, Bella explained that his big back grinding teeth were few and not good enough for big carrots, so he had a mix of senior feed and the cookies he loved, and shredded carrots Amber prepared for him every day. She mixed in mints, and candy sticks which he sucked like a straw now that it was hard for his back teeth to meet and crunch them up. There was a sign near the bucket of treats, that said "feed only in his little dish"!

The old horse reached his head out eagerly to a small dish Bella showed Keiya how to fill and hold. Bella said that his teeth were so long in the front, that he often got fingers confused with the food, and it was better not to feed him by hand. Only Amber still ruffled his mane and fed him with the flat of her hand. She was quick enough to save her fingers most of the time. Bella told her Amber had a couple of broken knuckles from not being quick enough. Amber had ridden him until two years before, he had just looked back as if to say "nope, not anymore" and tried to buck Amber off. She rode him a little while bareback, to make sure, but he seemed to be relieved when she stopped, so he no longer was ridden except by small children while being led by a horsehandler.

Bella laughed, she said Amber also got stuck on him bareback and had to grab on to a roof eave and ease herself on to a fence, her back had gotten stuck from one of her car accident injuries. Amber, Bella told Keiya no longer rode the horses because she could not make her one leg move properly to get off. She did not think it was safe to get stuck on a horse, but she still trained from the "downsy" side.

Bella was teaching Keiya words about horses and the stable. She found out the "outriders" were often called other names by other programs, but Amber had called them "outriders" because they, like the outriders at the track, came along side the horses and riders for safety. The outriders all had silk jackets and special tee shirts that said "outrider" on them. Sometimes the outriders walked beside the horse to help the rider as needed, others rode a horse on either side (sometimes two riders, one on each side) to be there for riders who were getting more independent but still might need help in balance. She told Keiya that some of the riders rode with one horse on one side, the rider leading the horse of the student, with another outrider on the other side to make sure the student did not fall. The outriders and their horses were specially trained with training dummies to not get upset if a person fell on, or towards them since their job was to push in and let their rider grab the student safely.

The girls wandered out to the grouping of round corrals. Bella told her that the small group and private lessons were all taught in the round corrals so Amber, or the other main instructors could reach out and grab the horse if necessary. They stopped to watch as a young boy was pushed in his wheelchair into one of the round corrals where a horse was waiting with his handler and two outriders. As he was wheeled up, he reached out and touched the horse on the neck, the horse knelt on one knee, his leg nearest the boy stretched out along the ground, the boy grabbed the strange strap wrapped around the horse and put his right leg on the horse's back, across the pad. Then he clicked a small sound and the horse rose slowly to standing. The boy adjusted himself and the handler led him off to walk around the rails of the corral. Bella told Keiya the strap was called a vaulting circingle and the pad was a special vaulting pad that had Velcro straps to hold it in place through the rings on the circingle made for that purpose.

Keiya was beside herself. She could now imagine herself really riding. Bella told her that many of the horses were trained to kneel for the wheelchair bound riders. She showed her the tags hanging on the halter of the horse, and said each horse had numbers and letters below their name that told the handlers what the horse was certified to do in programs. Bella told her that many of the handlers were the owners, who came to classes just for them, to learn to help their horse get accustomed to the walkers, canes, wheelchairs, and the big cranes necessary for a few very disabled riders.

Moving along to the big arena, Keiya saw a large group of riders, all riding without handlers or outriders. They were boys and girls of many ages. Bella told her that the big arena classes were for the independent riders who had gotten certified to ride alone. This class was from a foster care group home. The therapy involved in this class included art, music, dance, drama, and mentoring programs with volunteer teachers who spent time with small groups helping them catch up in school. Bella then showed her a large library like building with tables, computers, and shelves of books, art materials, and a small kitchen in the corner. There were cameras and lights along one corner wall. There was an old fashioned sign out front that said "The One Room School".

Bella told her they got to make their own videos that the students often put on the popular website UTube. The students liked to make videos of themselves making up music videos, or public service ads for many things, such as not littering, or taking care of animals, or helping each other in many ways. She said next time Keiya came, she would take time to show her some of the videos on the computer big screen that took up one whole wall of the large room.

Outside was a large area of picnic tables and an outdoor cooking stage for cooking classes. Bella said they got volunteers from famous restaurants all over the area to come and teach the classes. Bella said there was an ancient woman from a nearby church that came from time to time to cook a real southern barbequed chicken dinner. She laughed as she told of neighbors who smelled the good smell and called their friends and neighbors to come and buy a dinner. The woman was such a good cook she was a celebrity around the local area. The Grandfather of one of the riders had been a cook on a big Navy ship. He occasionally would host a fundraiser and make his famous "Daddy's Ribs". The riding student had called him "Daddy" even though he was her Grandfather, and she would tell the others that one day they would taste "Daddy's Ribs". She made them sound so good, they asked and asked, and she had gotten him to make some for the class. "Daddy" did not know how to make "just a few" ribs for a few riders. He brought out two big trays of ribs, and afterwards started doing the fundraising dinners. He would make greens, and either a spicy rice dish, or three cheese macaroni and cheese. The riders came free, but many community members came and paid donations for the programs just for the chance to take a class with a famous chef, or to eat with the fabulous volunteers fan club. It helped to pay for the hay and other costs of the programs.

Bella and Keiya next went to the pool and the several large hot spas. The sign over the gate indicated this was a therapeutic area as well. Bella told her that many of the programs used this form of therapy as group therapy substitutes because it helped the members more than sitting in chairs staring at each other. Several therapists rented out the space by the hour for their own programs. Bella showed her the high diving boards, and the trampolines with large rig supports for the students. The classes were all taught by professional level volunteers from a nearby Olympic training center. The classes helped young people deal with fear, and other issues no one would associate with swimming and diving. Some swimmers went on to the Special Olympic Swim teams after they completed training here.

The last place Bella showed Keiya was a neat little bungalow. It was roomy enough for the wheelchair to get through easily. Bella told her this was where some of the physical therapists who rented space and also taught some of the equine therapy programs taught their clients how to live independently as they got near an age where they would be leaving home. Keiya was very interested, she had never considered that she herself might someday grow up and live on her own. For the first time she began to think of her life as her own, not the life of her disabilities. Keiya told Bella this. Bella said, that happened to me here too. I used to think of myself as less, a "foster" child, and then, one day here, I realized I was just me, Bella, and God had not made me to be less, he had made me to be all that I can be, to stop limiting myself. Amber teaches that your first day. You will see. But it took me awhile to understand what she meant.

Bella asked Keiya if she wanted to come and help her teach a reading class. She explained that part of the programs here were for literacy. Many busloads of children from schools, scout programs, churches, temples and other youth programs came to learn about the fun of reading from the horses. Keiya wondered. She followed Bella to a covered small arena surrounded by bleachers. Children were pouring out of three school busses and up into the seats. A young man brought in a huge brown horse. He bowed to the children and took his place before a podium. Keiya, like all the others, was delighted.

The young man brought out a huge pair of glasses. Keiya could see they really had no glass in them, and put them on the horse's face. He had special straps that helped hold them up. He asked the children to open their books and read along. The young man read a book about a horse and a young girl who loved him very much, but some bad people stole the horse. The big brown horse turned the pages as the children turned the pages of the books they had in their laps. Every time he turned a page, the young man gave him a small treat. Sometimes he got too eager for his treat and turned the page too fast, and had to turn the page back so the young man could finish reading the words on the page. The children screamed with laughter. When the horse got away and came home, through his adventure, the children clapped and were very happy. The big brown horse bowed. Keiya recognized the signal to the horse as the same one given to the horse that had kneeled for the child in the wheelchair to mount.

"Well, here you are, and we have to hurry, or we will not get home in time to meet Dad to go to Grandmother's for dinner". Keiya wanted to whine, but she knew from the look on her Mom's face that she would be coming back. She said good-bye and thank you to Bella and Amber and rolled her electric wheelchair to the lift mount on the waiting van.

On the way home, Keiya was chattering and laughing and telling Mom everything she could remember of her day. For

ONCE, Mom did not have any music on, and the ride was over quickly as she told her everything she had seen and done. Dad was waiting in the driveway, and jumped into the van. The family started off, Mom with a glazed look on her face, and Dad now smiling and hearing the whole story all over again about the wonderful introduction to the horse ranch programs.

When Mom could get a word in, she told Dad that Amber had called Keiya's physical therapist and they had worked out a plan for the therapist to bring out several clients two times a week. Each client would have their own program set up by Amber and the physical therapist. Best of all, said Mom, Keiya can go straight from school with the others in the school van and we do not have to pay, it is on our insurance. Keiya told Dad that the best thing she had noticed was that no one had given her "that" look. Everyone had just said hi, or kept on what they were doing, no one cared that she was in a wheelchair. Dad and Mom smiled. They had listened too many times to Keiya's sadness when someone in school, or a store had let her know she was not just a person to say hi to and like, that she was different, and apart. They felt happy that Keiya had found a place to deal with this problem. The therapist and Amber had told Mom that dealing with other people was a big part of the program. It was, Mom told Dad, not about riding horses, it was about a whole lot more.

Keiya was so excited her first day. She wheeled to the school van that was going to take her to the ranch. She looked at the other children in the van and was surprised that she had not known this many of the students went to the horse program. As the van entered the gates, and the students began to unload, Keiya waited her turn impatiently. She saw Bella outside the van waiting for her. Bella said hi, and told her that for today, she would be her buddy. She explained that every time anyone came to the ranch they were given a buddy. The two were responsible to keep their eyes on each other and make sure both were always safe. The ranch was in a busy area, many workers came in and out, and it was important for each rider to be safe. Bella took her to the check in office where Keiya got her laminated identification tag to snap on the pocket of her new ranch shirt that had the logo and her name embroidered on the pocket.

Keiya asked Bella about so many kids from her school being on the van. Bella told her that many of the kids were there for literacy programs, to increase their reading, writing and other school skills. Many were there for group therapy or for anger management programs. Bella said that sometimes people are crippled inside in many ways that are not as obvious as when one is crippled outside.

The two had come to a small round corral. A tall girl in jeans and cowboy boots stood in the middle with a medium sized copper colored horse. Two other women, one about twenty and the other about fifty, leaned against the corral bars. All three wore the ranch shirts with their names embroidered on the pockets. Big Macs, the dog, stood nuzzling the horse.

As Keiya and Bella came into the corral, Bella introduced the horse, she showed Keiya how to hold her hand outstretched, palm down, for the horse to sniff. She explained this is the horsey handshake. Horses keep their knowledge in a big part, in the part of their brain that deals with smell, the horse will learn and recognize your smell, your sound, and the sound of your voice, as well as what you look like moving through space faster than you will recognize the horse. Keiya wondered what she meant. Someday she already had a secret dream of being as knowledgeable and helpful as Bella. Bella introduced her to the horse handler, the tall woman in western boots, and the two outriders. Keiya was so excited by the horse, who she had learned was named "Penny" because of her color, she immediately forgot the names she was told.

She apologized as she was reintroduced, and by the kind smiles, knew that each of them completely understood the horse was so overwhelming that it could cause a loss of manners.

Bella said she would be back in half an hour. That next time Keiya would begin to learn to get the horse ready for the class. She said Keiya would learn to catch and groom the horse. That "Penny" was used to wheelchairs. She, Bella would be there for every step of the process until Amber felt that Keiya was able to do it all alone. Then she would be assigned a buddy and the two would use the same horse for their class and be there to help and watch out for each other if necessary.

Amber came into the corral. She asked Keiya if she remembered how to greet "Penny". Keiya approached the horse in her motorized wheelchair as Bella had taught her, with her hand out, palm down and let "Penny" sniff and nuzzle the back of her hand. She then rubbed the end of the nose and side of her face with the back of her hand.

"Very nice," said Amber. "Now I want you to roll back along her side, right down here to me, Amber was standing behind the strap around "Penny's" girth.

"Rub your hand along her side as you come, and let her know where you are. She cannot see you at all, she can hear and feel you, and "Penny" is very experienced with new riders, but you still do not want to startle her.

Feeling scared, Keiya put her hand timidly on "Penny" and as the chair rolled towards Amber, she pulled her hand along the horse's neck and left it resting on the shoulder near the circingle.

"Now, turn the chair slowly, switch hands, and keep your hand on her shoulder"

Keiya did what Amber asked. The horse handler was now standing close to "Penny's" face, quietly talking to her. The horse stood perfectly still. The two outriders moved up on each side of the horse, one standing behind the wheelchair.

Amber tapped the horse gently on the near shoulder, almost on the left leg, and the horse extended her left leg, leaned back as her right leg bent beneath her body in one smooth move. Amber and the outrider helped Keiya put her right leg over the horse and use her hands on the vaulting rings on each side of the withers to pull herself upright. Keiya felt terrified.

"Just breathe a little" said Amber. "Relax, like a Raggedy Ann doll, just let your arms and legs hang and let your head droop on your chest, and breathe in slowly, hold it, and breathe out slowly.

It seemed as if she had been on the scary horse for a long time. Keiya could feel sweat trickling down her back she was so afraid. But she continued to listen to Amber's calm voice. The outrider had reached down and motored the chair out side the gate and returned to gently hold Keiya by her left thigh, the other outrider held her right thigh in the same manner. Amber had her hand on her back to steady her, and nodded to the horse handler. The horse handler made a small sound, and the horse swung effortlessly to a standing position. Keiya could not breathe. She seemed so high in the air.

"Just breathe," Amber repeated, and everyone was just quiet. The horse just stood, rock still, quietly breathing in and out. To Keiya the sound was like a roaring in her ears, and she felt every breath in and out under her legs. She wanted to shout to get her down, but Bella had told her, over and over, the horse does not know you are afraid of the horse, it just knows you are afraid, and might try to get out of the way of whatever is making you so afraid. Amber told her to close her eyes, and just breath with everyone. She could hear all the others breathe slowly in, hold it, and then slowly out. Finally she opened her eyes and loosened her grip on the vaulting handles.

Amber showed her how to loosen her leg grip around the horse. She told her that "Penny" was so experienced she did not get upset, but most horses, when gripped like that would get upset and prance around, or try to run away. "Never below the knees" Amber told her. Remember, never hold the horse with any part of your body below your knees.

She told Keiya about the arm and leg exercises she had seen the other riders doing, and then began to ask her to do them. "Penny" just stood quietly, not looking to right or left, as her handler gently continued to talk to her and stroke her face softly.

"Now, I want you to begin to say the alphabet, one letter to each hoofbeat. Listen closely and try to feel the hooves as they hit the ground, I want to hear the letter when the hoof hits the ground, not when you guess it is about to." The handler began to walk, the outriders walked along holding on to Keiya by both her knees. Bella had told her if a student became unbalanced the outriders could jump right in and use their hold on her legs to right her, and the horse handler would stop the horse until everything was safe again. Still, she felt terrified as the body of the horse swung into motion. She was trying to do the breathing exercises again when she remembered she was supposed to be saying the alphabet. She listened, as a hoof hit the ground, she said "a,".

By the end of the lesson Keiya could do all of the arm and leg exercises at the walk, and say the alphabet with ease. Amber said that was enough for today, and she would teach Keiya to dismount, and thank her horse. Bella had already showed Keiya how to "give the horse cookies" which meant to rub in little circles on the neck or shoulder and say "good". Amber told her that "Penny" liked being told "Good Penny" as she liked to hear her own name.

When the horse was standing perfectly still, the horse handler close to her face and rubbing her nose, the outrider maneuvered the chair into place. Amber and the other outrider held Keiya by her lower legs as Amber told her how it was going to work for her to dismount. First, Amber asked "Penny" to kneel again. The horse kneeled smoothly. The outrider stood on the left of "Penny" as Amber, Keiry and the right outrider helped Keiya to slide backwards towards the wheelchair. They helped her put one foot on the ground, and sit in the chair. Then to pull her other leg off the horse and into the foot rests of the chair. The horse handler, when signaled by Amber, signaled the horse to rise, and they moved to the side. Keiya straightened herself in the chair and fastened the seat belt. Amber told her to go back and thank "Penny". She gave her a handful of carrot bites and a mint to give to "Penny". Keiya, as Bella had taught her, extended the treats in her hand towards the horse's nose, and as she nuzzled and ate them, told "Penny" what a "good Penny" she was. The handler took the horse out the gate, and Keiya left with Bella to go to her next class. The hot tub therapy group!

As Bella and Keiya laughed and got into their swimsuits with the help of the aides in the changing room, Keiya wondered what this class would be like. As she rolled out into the pool area, she saw that one of the therapy pools had a line of wheelchairs, some electric, like hers, and some non-motorized were by the pool. A small elderly lady with sunglasses on and her tee shirt with the logo on over a swimsuit was holding the control on a crane and helping the students who could not get out of their chairs and into the pools with the help of aides get into the water. Each of the seats in the tub had rails along the sides so the students could steady themselves in the warm bubbly water if necessary. Keiya looked at the other students as she waited her turn to be helped into the pool. They were all girls about her own age. First the lady, who introduced herself as Ms. Lily, led them in exercises in the water. Then she got a little beach ball and tossed it to one of the students. She explained as she tossed it, when you get the ball, tell us your name, tell us that you are wonderful because God created you, and tell us something very wonderful about you.

I will start. Ms. Lily told them she was wonderful because she had once been an Olympic swimmer, but gotten cancer and had to stop sports. She had recovered and gone on to become a coach in a swim team at a school for very rich girls. She had at first felt sorry for herself, she wanted to be an Olympic Gold Medalist, but that part of her life was over from all the surgery and chemo. Then she realized that no matter how much money her students had, they still needed a good coach to love and encourage them. Now she was retired and volunteered here with the physical and other therapists. Everyone looked at the girl with the ball, who began to tell her story. Each of the girls, as the ball was tossed to them told their story. Keiya noticed that not one of them mentioned their disability as they all had noticed that Ms. Lily had not mentioned her missing arm.

Keiya began to love her program and began to be happier at school. She had simply never noticed other disabled children. She had felt she was the only one, that everyone was always staring at her, laughing, or looking at her with pity, or worse "that look", the one that made her feel like less. Now, as she and others talked about these things in the bubby little pool, she began to smile at other students, and ask if they would like to come after school and join her and others for a movie or trip to the video game-house in the mall, or even to her birthday party. She was excited to have her first ever birthday party with friends from school. Bella and others from the stable came too.

One day Amber told her to say a special good-bye and thank you to "Penny" because her next class she would be moving in to a group class that could ride better. Keiya had not even realized that one week at a time she had needed less and less balancing help from the outriders. She had not realized that she was able to kneel on the horse with only a reassuring hand on either knee. She no longer needed Amber to jump up behind her and hold her when she stretched tall on her knees. She had not even noticed that she was much more able to get around her own house without the wheelchair. Moving from bed, to chair without the chair, leaning on the furniture for balance and to support her legs.

As she gave a special treat to "Penny" she nuzzled her face and hair against the soft nose and started to cry. She was going to miss the horse. "You can still go by and give her a treat in her stall," said Amber with a pat on her shoulder.

That evening as Keiya sat looking around her room, she noticed how many of her old horse pictures were replaced with framed pictures of her and "Penny". In one picture she and Bella were smiling as they finished the braids for a show event at the ranch. "Penny" was covered with ribbons and flowers woven into the braids on her mane and tail. Keiya thought about how much more fun it was to groom and ride a real horse than to sit and look at her carousel horses. She realized she had missed many episodes of the horse channel shows.

Show day had arrived. A big show, for a fundraising event was taking place that afternoon at the big horseshow arena across the county. The big horse vans had come that morning to pick up the horses for the show. Bella had told her this was her first year to get to drive out with the vans, trailers, and Amber and the other instructors and trainers.

When Keiya got to the horseshow arena, Mom and Dad were directed where to take her to unload out of the van. Bella met her at that gate, and gave Mom and Dad their tickets after telling them the directions of where to park the van. Keiya and Bella went into the big, lush barns and found the horses they were going to be getting ready for the show. Keiya had a bag of flowers, ribbons and some feathers she had gotten as a present from her Aunt who could not make it to the show from the far off rez. The girls, and other riders laughed and talked as they brushed the horses shiney. Bella taught her how to put on special show spray that had glitter in it so the horse's hooves would be sparkly in the lights of the arena. Each horse was sprayed with a tiny spray bottle and Bella showed her how to make beautiful designs in the hair with a tiny tined comb. Then they sprayed a quick mist of hair spray out of a mister to hold the design.

Some of the riders where using saddles, others were using circingles. Keiya was riding with a western saddle. She had worked hard with another kneeling horse "Sneakers" an old show horse who had been donated when his young owner left for college. She said she wanted to come back on vacations and volunteer and see "Sneakers". As she brushed and braided "Sneakers" she was so excited she felt like it was her first day of riding again.

She remembered the television show so many months ago, when this had all started. Now, here she was, her dream come true. She braided the ribbons, and flowers into the mane and tail, then using the threads her mother had tied on to the feathers, she tied the fluttering feathers on to the forelock, mane and tail of "Sneakers". The beautiful brown horse, with his striking black legs and black mane and tail looked beautiful. Amber came and led her to the arena gate.

She heard the announcer say "Keiya and 'Sneakers' will show us the third level western riding program."

Keiya motored her chair in to the arena where "Sneakers" was standing quietly. He was not bothered by the people and all the lights. She was. As she went up and nuzzled his face to say hello, she felt his quiet strength and calmed down. She tapped his shoulder and he kneeled so she could throw her right leg over and pull herself into the saddle. It had taken months practicing by the big barrel with a saddle that stood in one of the side yards at the ranch to be able to do this, but she had been determined. When firmly in the saddle, she made a quiet sound, and "Sneakers" glided to his feet, waiting for the signal from his handler. The handler handed Keiya the reins, and held only the long lounge line.

Keiya gave the signal to walk and she and the horse went out to the end of the line and began to circle to music she had chosen. She then asked the horse to trot, and finally to canter. As the music played, she felt like she could see herself, a tiny figure, on a horse covered with flowers, feathers and ribbons going in magical circles. She signaled the horse to a walk, then stop. Someone brought her wheelchair up as she gave the signal for "Sneakers" to kneel. She dismounted, and after fastening herself into her chair, thanked the horse. She and "Sneakers" turned to the crowd as they applauded and shouted for her.

On the drive home, all Keiya could think of was that fanciful fairy waltz of her horse and herself with ribbons, flowers, and feathers flapping in the wind.

That night, going to sleep, Keiya smiled at her favorite carousel, as the lighted merry-go- round circled to the melody of the music box. It was the only one with tiny figures on each small horse. Keiya had given each rider a name from someone in her riding group.

Carousel Horse-a screenplay

A carousel turns. The tinkling music plays, the nightlight in the small carousel illuminates the tiny figures on the tiny horses. A teenager sleeps quietly in the room that is plastered with posters, and pictures of carousels and carousel horses. On the bedstand is a picture of the girl with a man standing beside her holding her on the carousel horse of some park somewhere.

Fade:

The girl is waking up, she struggles to the edge of the bed.

Kieya

Mom, Mom. I need to get up.

A woman, disheveled, and obviously just waking up comes into the room. She moves to the bed, and with obvious experience expertly helps Kieya get into the wheelchair and pushes her towards the bathroom.

Fade:

Kieya is watching television. On the screen a horseshow is just ending, the beautiful jumping horse completes his round, the final scores are flashed on the screen and the program ends. The next show begins. A young man in a wheelchair is pushed into an arena as the credits roll. Kieya leans towards the television. The young man is helped to mount the horse, then rides off alone and does a western routine, ending to shattering applause from the crowd. He rides out of the arena towards a person with his waiting wheelchair.

A group of youngsters in wheelchairs enters the arena, several horses are led in. Fade:

The young man from the televised horse show rides his horse to his handler, who snaps a lead line on and leads the horse to where a medium sized woman stands with his wheelchair. She claps her hands and gives him the thumbs up. She is smiling widely at him.

Amber

Great job, Kenny. You really earned that applause

A very well suited somewhat tense man is walking through the crowd and approaches them from behind. Kenny cannot see him, but Amber has full view

Kenny

Did you see my Dad? He was finally proud of me. He has never been proud of me before.

Now he knows.......I can do something good.

Amber watches as the tense man stops, listens and starts to cry. He pulls a handkerchief out of his immaculate suit and wipes his eyes.

Father

Kenny, Dad has always been proud of you.

It is unmistakable that both he and Kenny know that is not true.

Fade:

Kieya's Mom is in the kitchen, she is banging dishes and pots as she loads the dishwasher, she has LOUD rock music playing. A shattering scream "MOM" causes her to drop a dish, and rush out of the kitchen, to the room where Kieya is watching television intently.

Kieya

MOM, look at this!

Can I find a place to learn this?

Mom

If we can find a place…………

She does not sound happy.

Keiya

I know we can.

She turns the chair to the nearby desk and clicks on her computer and begins to search.

Keiya

Look, here is one, it is in our town, but I do not
recognize the street.

Mom moves over to peer over her shoulder at the screen.

Mom

That is just outside of town.......

Keiya

(interrupting) Can I go, can we go today!
Can we?

Mom

We have to call them.

Keiya looks at the computer screen, grabs the phone and dials.
Hands the phone to her Mother.

Mom talks quietly into the phone, nodding and jots down
something on a piece of paper.

Keiya

Can we? Can we? Can we go today?

Mom

Yes, they are open six days a week, and we can
come right out.

Keiya and Mom gather together things, and go to the garage, where Mom helps Keiya into the electric wheelchair so she can wheel herself out to the van and get on to the lift to get going.

They set out and turn on to the freeway.

Keiya is so excited. She shouts over the LOUD rock music Mom is playing while driving.

Keiya

How far is it? Do you think I can ride a horse today? Have you ever ridden a horse?

Mom reaches down and turns the music volume up higher, ignoring her daughter. Keiya just keeps on shouting her questions, and looking out the windows eagerly.

The van exits the freeway and begins to roll along a two lane road which soon is populated on both sides by small horse ranches and houses that have one or two stalls visible from the street.

Mom turns down the music and begins to pay attention to the directions the GPS system is giving her. The system announces they have arrived just as Keiya screams another curdling scream of excitement.

Keiya

This is IT! We are here. I can't wait.

Mom moves into a parking spot and help Keiya unload from the van. A young teen is standing watching. She walks up to Keiya.

Bella

Hi, I am Bella, are you Keiya? We have been expecting you.

Mom finishes locking up the van, then walks up to the two girls.

Keiya

Yes, and this is my Mom. Mrs. Brandon. Mom, this is Bella.

Mrs. Brandon

Nice to meet you Bella, do you live here?

Bella

OH, I wish. No, I am a volunteer. I will be Keiya's buddy for today. Let's go find Amber, she is the Director, and Trainer. She is expecting you two.

They walk, and wheel along and find a medium sized woman, well over fifty, just finishing a class in a round pen. After the horses, with their handlers, then the students in their wheelchairs, or with their walkers leave the small corral, Amber walks to them with her hand out. She walks with a limp, but is sunny spirited and friendly.

Amber

Takes a little longer to get myself in motion. I can walk much better as I get around a bit.

Bella, can you stay today. We might need a
little extra help.

A young woman in the same tee shirt with the stable logo as
Bella and Amber is seen coming down the pathway with a
small copper colored horse. As they walk past other students
some call out to the little horse

Students

Hello Penny. Good Penny.

The horse flickers her ears at them, but does not turn her head
or change her pace as she follows her handler into the small
pen where Amber is holding the gate. Amber closes the gate
after two more young women in stable tee shirts enter and
stand on either side of Penny. The handler is standing directly
to the left front of Penny's nose, petting her and quietly talking
to her. The horse stands completely still.

A young boy in a motorized wheelchair similar to Keiya's
is waiting outside the gate. He seems a little bit afraid. His
Mother is standing beside him talking to him quietly.

Amber

Bella, tell Keiya and Mrs. Brandon the safety
rules for each time they enter the round corral
for a class.

As Bella talks, she watches the young boy approach the horse
with hand outstretched, and then run his hand down the
horse's neck as he motors down to the front shoulder and faces
the horse.

Amber moves to the young boy, and helps him maneuver his chair through the last part. He glances back at this Mother apprehensively.

The handler and the outriders position themselves. Amber taps the horse on her lower left shoulder, the horse gracefully extends her left leg, and bends her right into a bow.

Bella

First, always listen to the handlers, or Amber.

Second, never believe movies or books. Horses are horses. They can, no matter how docile they seem, turn into a bucking bronc from a rodeo. Always follow the safety rules.

If you are afraid, tell Amber, or your instructor quietly.

No parents are allowed in the ring. The handlers know how to deal with emergencies. Parents just get in the way and get hurt, or cause someone else to get hurt.

Third, horses here are trained for this type of work, and chosen for each lesson because Amber and the horse handlers have agreed the horse is ready to work safely for that class. Horses are just like people, the handlers know which side of the stall they got up on. Sometimes a horse needs some special exercise, or just a day off. The horse handlers decide that with Amber. Do not throw tantrums if your favorite horse is not there for your class.

Amber wrote the book on the first five hundred hours of Nativeamerican horsemanship. She will teach you step by step. You are NOT going to be a movie kid galloping down the beach or through the mountains today, next week, or maybe ever. Amber will guide your riding career for what is safe for you and the horse.

When we go through the gate, I will show you how to approach the horse.

Every time you approach a horse, that is the only way. Amber and the horse handlers are here to make sure you are safe, and the horses are treated respectfully and humanely. Just because they are bigger, does not mean they are not afraid of you. Many of the horses have had bad experiences before coming here. Until you have proven yourself, you are just another nightmare waiting to happen to them.

Keiya is bending her body as close to the fence as she can without falling out of the wheelchair, the safety strap is straining to keep her from falling out. She peers through the bars intently as the staff help the young boy slide his right leg over the horses blanket pad, and help him grasp the handles of the strap that is cinched tightly right behind his front legs. He pulls himself up and sits. Amber is talking quietly to him, the handler makes a small sound, and Penny glides back to a standing position. She stands perfectly still while the young boy looks down in what is easily seen as terror. The outriders each have a hand on one of his knees, and Amber uses her arms to brace him in the sitting position.

The horsehandler just continues to stand, petting the horse's face and talking quietly to her.

Keiya can see the boy begin to breathe deeply and smile at comments from Amber she cannot hear. Soon he is pointing to the parts of the horse, and then raising his arms over his head, putting his hand on his shoulders, on his knees, and on his hips as directed.

Bella is explaining the process to her, but Keiya is oblivious to either Bella, or her Mother.

The little boy begins to copy Amber as she rubs tiny circles on the horse's shoulder.

Bella

Those are "horsey cookies". Like a thank you, and well done, and I trust you all in one. It is important to learn about "horsey cookies".

Keiya is rubbing her hands in small circles on her lap as she continues to stare through the bars of the corral.

In a moment she sees the small boy saying something and the horse is walking slowly and with careful measured steps around the edges of the corral. When they get near enough, Keiya hears him saying the alphabet.

Bella

Saying the alphabet helps him calm down and learn to pay attention to the horse's hoof beats.

Sometime soon he will begin to have numbers
and math problems that go to the sound of each
hoof beat as well. It depends on each rider.

The little boy continues to ride and all too soon for Keiya
comes to a stop. He rubs the horse with the learned "horsey
cookies" while the left side outrider motors his wheelchair
back to him. Amber touches the horse on the left shoulder
again. The horse bows and the staff help him to dismount
back to his wheelchair. He motors to the front of the horse,
giving her some rubs on her nose and then a flat hand filled
with treats Amber has just given him from a small bag in her
pocket.

After the little boy and his mother have gone, and Penny and
her handler have walked on down the path, Amber approaches
Mrs. Brandon and Keiya where they are still with Bella
outside the corral.

Keiya

Am I going to get to do that?

Can I?

She looks eagerly from Amber to Mrs. Brandon.

Amber

I can't make you a promise until I see the
orders from your doctor and therapists.

You may work with your own therapists, many
of them from town come out on certain days to
do their own classes with their regular patients.

Some doctors and therapists have me, or one of
my instructors do the class for them. We send
them a report each time the rider comes.

But, if they all say yes, then I can promise you
I will do all I can to see that you can do as
much as is safe and healthy for you.

We also never make anyone go farther than
they are ready to, so keep that in mind when
you get scared.

Your Mom and I are going to go talk, and call
your doctors and therapists. You go with Bella,
she will show you the rest of the ranch.

The two women walk away towards the office, chatting, Bella
leads the way towards the stables, Keiya following in her
wheelchair.

Fade:

The two girls enter the first of the barns. As they approach
heads pop out of the stalls and whinnies and rumbles sound.
Keiya is a bit afraid.

Bella

They are just saying hi, give us a treat.

She shows Keiya a big bag of carrots in the tackroom as the
enter the barn. She shows her how to break the carrots into
small portions and hold just one piece on the flat of her hand
and extend it to the horse. They come to the first stall and
Bella shows her how to feed the horse the carrot. The other

horses continue to make sounds and push their noses out of the stalls.

Keiya is still nervous, but wheels up to a horse, puts a carrot piece on her palm and extends her hand. The horse nuzzles into her hand, and chomps up the carrot. He looks for more.

Keiya gives him a few more pieces.

The two girls move down the barn feeding carrot pieces. Bella is describing the horses to Keiya.

Bella

This barn is filled with horses who belong to private owners. Amber does not want to get a group of horses left without hope if something should happen to the Foundation.

She gives the owners free board and hay. They all provide their own tack and supplements. They all use their horses regularly for their own use. Many of the horses are performance show horses of different kinds.

Most of the owners also donate time and money if they can to the Foundation. When any student gets to the place they can take private riding lessons in a performance sport with one of the performance rider/owners they can make their own arrangements. We have several performance trainers here.

All of the riding members in special programs can sign up for free additional performance riding programs if Amber and their doctors say it is safe. The trainers give the free lessons in exchange for free board and feed.

The girls have crossed to another barn. An old white horse leans out to Bella and nickers to her as she rubs his face.

Bella

This is Snow. He is 39 years old. That is like a 135 year old person.

He used to be an Arabian quarter mile race horse, the was put out to stud for more than ten years. He stopped producing live foals due to a tumor, so they threw him into the auction. He was not able to be trained, so went to another auction to be sold down.

Before he was picked him up for the auction, Amber bought him. She had exercised him for some months bareback in a small round corral and he lived in the pen next to one of her horses, so she saved his life. He has been working with her ever since.

Keiya

What is this?

She looks into a small bucket on a hook outside the stall where Snow could not reach it.

Beside the tub is an even smaller feeding tub hanging from a strap.

Bella

That is his favorite treat. Most of his back
grinding teeth either do not meet, or are gone,
so he can not chew big carrot pieces. Amber
makes him this pail everyday so he can have
treats too. His front teeth are so long, he often
gets fingers by mistake, so always use the
feeding bowl with a handful of the mix. It is
cookies, mints, and shredded carrots mixed
with senior horse feed.

She shows Keiya how to toss a handful into the little bowl and
hold it while the old horse gobbles it.

Keiya takes the bowl and tosses another handful into the little
bowl and feeds the horse.

Fade:

The girls have reached the pool. Inside the pool area are a
large Olympic sized pool, several levels of diving boards.
Along one side is a trampoline with cable suspension system
for divers.

Keiry

What is all that?

Bella

It is a real Olympic level training center for
diving. Most of our swimming instructors are
Red Cross Certified Life Guards, but they are
also athletes from the Olympic training center

on the other side of town. They volunteer
time here to teach all levels of swimming and
diving. Some of the coaches volunteer for
special exhibition classes where the students
show their skills and teach other students
new ones. The events have a barbeque and
are fundraisers for the ranch to keep up the
swimming and pool areas.

The girls have reached the area where several large whirlpool
therapy pools are clustered. There is a line of youths, some in
walkers, some in wheelchairs waiting for the two instructors
to help them into the water. A couple of others, in motorized
chairs are waiting by a crane system to be lifted out of the
chairs and into the pool.

As they get ready to go into the pool, each of the students
sheds their stable tee shirt and has only a swim suit
underneath. Some of the students are helped in to floatation
jackets.

Keiya looks at Bella.

Bella

Some students have so much problem with
balance, and have not learned how to swim
well enough, so they wear boating type life
saving floatation vests in the pools and spas.

Keiya nods, and turns back to watch the class.

The instructor tells them to do a series of exercises. They all
follow. The other instructor assists one or two of the students
as needed.

Keiya

Who are all those students?

A new group has come in the gate and are sliding into the water to begin warm up exercises. A young instructor is talking to them as they enter the water.

Bella

Those are the foster kids from a couple of group homes. The staff over there on the benches has to come with them and watch them the whole time they are here.

Keiya watches the new group finish their warm up and begin to line up by the diving boards, and a small group by the trampoline.

Bella

I was in one of those group homes once.

Keiya looks at her with interest. The two girls continue to watch the others.

Bella

It was really hard at first. Now I just tell people. It is part of my reality. Amber says we have to accept our reality to overcome it.

The horses helped me. So many of them have been abandoned, or abused. It helped me to realize that I could move on with my life too.

Keiya

Laughing

You know what? I was so jealous of you when I got here. I thought you had everything I wanted. Horses, and legs that work and a great place to live.

Bella

And I was jealous of you. I knew you had a Mom and Dad, and had no idea until I saw you roll out of the van that you were disabled.

I wonder how many others I have been jealous of that really have something in their reality that would make me know I do not have to be jealous, just their friend.

The two girls laugh and hug each other.

Keiya

Do you think Amber sent you to meet me, and to spend the day with me for just this reason.

The two girls laugh again and go back to watching the other kids with more joy.

As the swimmers begin to gather their things and head for the outdoor showers along one wall, the two girls head out the gate of the swimming area.

Bella

Let's go find something to eat. We have a cooking area.

If we are lucky, they will still be cooking.

Looking at her watch.

I think we are in time for lunch.

Keiya follows along in her chair as Bella heads quickly up and down paths between the barns and other program sites. The pair come to an outdoor kitchen area. Sixty or so youths and staff are sitting on benches at small picnic tables watching a cooking demonstration.

The tables in the front, with about twenty students, are preparing food along with the chef who is teaching the class.

The chef, Keiya recognizes from the cable cooking network. She is excited to watch her cook right here, in front of the students. The chef and staff walk along the tables where students are cooking, correcting and demonstrating.

Soon, big salads are ready. The chef has taken a giant cheese wheel and some hard boiled eggs to the tables, where the students crack, clean and slice the eggs, and grate cheese to put on top of the big bowls of salad.

Chef

Time to eat.

The students who cooked serve the others. While some are going up front to serve, others expertly pass out dishes,

napkins and silverware. Two pass out glasses, and another pair
walk behind serving lemonade.

Bella

The lemonade is made with lemons we grow
here, and also mint that is grown in our own
gardens. I will take you there after lunch.

Keiya follows Bella to the front where she is served salad and
beautiful multi- grain rolls.

Bella

We do not grow the grain here, but we eat
whole grain in all our homemade breads, rolls,
pancakes and waffles. We have breakfast on
fundraising weekend days.

Everyone is laughing and eating.

Keiya

Everyone gets along here. It is not like school
where the kids are all in separate groups and
some are so mean. I have not heard any mean
kids here.

Bella

Amber does not allow it. It is hard for some of
the kids when they get here.

I remember one kid.......

Fade.

An expensive car rolls up through the ranch gate.

Bella and Amber are standing with a group of children waiting. The driver emerges and after a seeming struggle convinces a small, wiry boy to exit.

Coming out of the vehicle, the boy glares at the others. They are smiling at him.

Cameron

What are you looking at?

You bunch of geeks?

I should kick your ass.

The other children look amazed. Amber approaches the boy.

Amber

That is unacceptable behavior here.

If you ask me, taking a good careful look at the others, I see YOU are the geek, not them.

The driver turns his face and smiles.

Cameron

I did not ask you, you old witch.

He kicks at Amber, who expertly grabs his foot. He slaps at her, she grabs his wrist. He slaps with the other hand, and that two is held by her firm grip. He attempts to kick her with his one free foot, and is left dangling from her outstretched arms. The other children smile, but none of them laughs. The boy is now raging in an uncontrolled tantrum.

Amber continues to hold him, motioning the driver back with a wag of her head in "no".

She says nothing.

Cameron continues to swear, scream and thrash. Finally he is quiet. Hanging by his wrists and ankles from Amber's hands.

Amber

If you promise to stop, and apology politely, I will let you go.

Cameron starts the show again.

When he is quiet, hanging once again from her hands, he speaks.

Cameron

I promise to stop. I apologize.

Amber immediately releases him gently to the ground, where he sits sullenly.

She turns to the others.

Amber

We have a new student, he is going to live with us for two weeks. This is Cameron, please introduce yourselves in the appropriate way, then he will introduce himself.

One by one the children step forward and introduce themselves.

Bella

Hello, My name is Bella, I am wonderful because God created me, I am also wonderful because I live in a foster home with two people who love me and take care of me now that my Mom and Dad can not.

As each of the children goes through the process, Cameron gives up the sullen look and begins to show interest.

April

Hello, My name is April, I am wonderful because God created me, I am also wonderful because when my Dad died in the war, I took care of my Mom and my little brother.

My Mom is remarried now, and they have, I mean we have, (she smiles tentatively at Amber, who smiles in return)

a new baby sister. I am wonderful because I love her and do not hate it anymore that she gets a mom and dad, and I have lost my mom and dad. I know my mom is my mom and my step dad is for me, not just her.

Cameron listens intently to the children by this point.

Amber

Cameron? It is your turn to introduce yourself.

The small boy squirms, but seems to win an inner battle.

Cameron

My name is Cameron. I am.........(he hesitates, it is obviously a struggle for him to go on.

The other children smile, and murmur encouragement to him.

I am wonderful because God created me.

He looks directly at Amber.

AM I wonderful, I have a different religion.

Amber

I believe that God, like breath, is something we all need. Like the word breath, it is different in many languages, and yet, without it, we are not able to survive.

Some people do not believe in God. I believe that is OK, and they are as wonderful as anyone else. Whether science, or nature, each of us in the only one of us we will ever be. Even if they cloned us, each clone would see different things, hear different things, and be one and only that person. I think that is what makes us wonderful.

Cameron nods and continues.

Cameron

I am wonderful because I have a birth defect that I have overcome. I am glad to be here with you.

He smiles at Amber and the children.

I have never had a friend.

People make fun of me because I look funny and walk funny.

Sometimes I hate myself because I know I look and walk funny.

The others begin to look at him, and then talk to him.

James

Well, one thing, I don't want to make you mad, but how come you have Velcro shoes?

And your shirt looks like a kindergarden kid.

Cameron begins to get mad, but sees Amber's look.

Cameron

My Mom and Grandmother buy all my clothes.

I am small, so they say I am their little boy, and I cannot tie my shoes, so Velcro. The kids at school make fun of me for the shirts and shoes.

James

We can teach you to tie your shoes.

And you need to tell your Dad to tell them that
you are going shopping with him from now on.

The other kids nod. James even sticks his foot out, unties his
shoe, and shows Cameron how to tie it. The kids take turns
getting Cameron to tie shoes.

The young people lead Cameron to the pool area and begin
taking off their stable tee shirts. They have swimwear
underneath. They shower in the outdoor showers along the
outside wall of the restrooms.

Cameron is hanging back and refusing.

Amber

Your Mom says you have a pool at home.

Why don't you want to swim?

Cameron

You can't make me swim.

I know how to swim.

I just don't want to.

The others have jumped into the pool and are doing their
warm up exercises with their swim instructor.

Amber grabs up Cameron, as if he is no heavier than a baby, and walks to the pool stairs. She descends the stairs, with the wailing and swearing Cameron and wades out into the middle of the pool where the water is about to her shoulders.

Cameron is hanging on desperately. Still screaming and swearing.

Amber simply stands there. Eventually Cameron calms down. Amber quiets him and has him lay back on his back, his legs dragging, soon he is smiling at her.

The others are just going on with their lesson, paying no attention to Cameron. Amber now has him on his tummy, she is holding him by his upper arms. He is kicking the water, and begins to put his face in the water, then blow big air bubbles, then out of the water and gulp air.

One of the instructors brings out a kickboard. Amber holds the board in the middle, and teaches Cameron to hold the board and kick his feet. He is obviously scared again.

The kids see him as Amber releases him and swims in front of him. He is kicking and thrashing, but the little kickboard keeps his face above water, and he is finally smiling as the others begin to root for him.

Cameron joins the others at the side and begins to take part in the class, his soggy tee shirt still clinging to him.

James

How come you don't just take that thing off?

Cameron

The other kids always made fun of me being so skinny, and funny looking, so, I don't like to swim. I quit swimming lessons because the kids were too mean.

Jennifer

They used to make fun of me too. I had cancer, and the chemo made me really fat. It hurt a lot, but my Mom went to the swimming class and told them about my cancer and asked them to help other kids with that kind of cancer by having a fundraiser.

They did, and invited a lot of cancer patients from the children's cancer program to come and have a swim and barbeque. A lot of them were fat with chemo, and some were very skinny and bald from their chemo.

The kids all got people to sign cards to promise they would not make fun of people because they do not know what their reality is. The people paid for the cards, and raised a lot of money. My Mom took the cards to work and sold them to every single person in her building.

A lot of them said they did not know that her daughter had been through cancer, and they wished they had been more helpful to our family.

Come on, take off the shirt.

The chubby little girl, in her swimsuit, with no tee shirt holds out her hand for the shirt. Cameron pulls it off and hands it to her, and starts back swimming with his kickboard, this time without Amber.

The children all cheer.

Fade:

The children are cooking breakfast, it is early in the morning. Some are mixing pancakes in large mixing bowls, others are cutting up fruit. Some are pouring milk into glasses and setting the table.

Cameron is looking with wonder as James pulls out a really nice pair of tennis shoes and a couple of shirts from his pack.

James

I only wore these a couple of times before my feet were too big, you can learn more about tying them, and take them home to show your Mom what you want.

Cameron hangs back.

Cameron

I don't think my Mom would like me wearing someone else's clothes and shoes.

James

We are friends here. You don't have a brother, I don't have a brother, she would not mind if you shared clothes with your brother.

Amber smiles thankfully at James.

Cameron

No.........probably not.......

He puts on one of the shirts, and the shoes. He has trouble with the laces, but is able to tie them finally.

Cameron models for the other kids.

They all applaud

Cindy

Yesterday, you said you had no friends, now you have all of us.

James

Amber, after breakfast, can we show him the computer room and how to keep in touch with us when he goes home?

Amber

That would be a really nice plan, then we will go ride. The kids attack their pancakes and fresh fruit.

Fade:

Cameron, changed, in new clothes, his tying shoes, and with a new attitude of confidence is with the children waiting for his ride.

As the car pulls up, the driver moves to get out and open the door. Cameron has already leapt forward, opened the door and thrown his things into the car interior. He turns and waves good-bye to his friends. Cameron jumps in the car and as the vehicle drives up the drive towards the road, his head pops out and he shouts good-bye to the waving and shouting students.

Fade:

Bella is checking the computer. Keiya is in her wheelchair beside her at the computer, she watches Bella check the account for the stable. There is an email from Cameron.

Bella

We got an email from Cameron. He says he has a new friend, a boy no one liked much, so he told him to come and go to lunch with him. They are having a lot of fun, and even making friends with other students.

He says his Dad told his Mom and Grandmother they cannot buy him clothes any more. That his friend is one he told about them, who said he would help him go and buy clothes. They had a lot of fun shopping with his Dad. His friend is a foster child who does not know where his Dad is.

The two girls smile, and Bella taps out an answer to Cameron.

Fade:

Keiya and Mrs. Brandon are driving in the van. The vehicle turns in to a medical building parking lot. Mrs. Brandon helps Keiya exit the powered lift system that brings her chair out of the van and to the ground.

The two enter the medical building and go into a doctor's office.

Mrs. Brandon takes a seat in the waiting room after checking in with the receptionist. Keiya moves her wheelchair close to her mother.

Keiya

Do you think he is going to OK my riding and swimming?

Mrs. Brandon

I have told you Keiya, I do not know. I do not think the doctor will know either until he orders some tests and gets them back.

The nurse appears at a door.

Nurse

Keiya Brandon.

Keiya and Mrs. Brandon move towards the door. The nurse directs them into a small office. The doctor walks in.

                    Dr. Overman

Mrs. Brandon, Keiya, it is good to see you. I
understand, Keiya, that you want to change
some of your physical therapy for the program
out at Amber's ranch?

Keiya nods.

                    Dr. Overman

I have had several patients with Amber's
programs over the years. I have two physical
therapists that work with her, if your test results
show it will not harm you, you can choose
either of them to work with.

Mrs. Brandon, the therapists send me a one
sheet observation each time Keiya goes to the
ranch. I bill the insurance company and pay
them directly. Amber always takes what the
insurance company pays, she does not charge
you a deductible.

I would ask that if you are able, you donate
some additional funds, or help with the
fundraisers. Horses and that big pool of hers
cost a lot to run, and she does not turn people
away because they can not pay.

Mrs. Brandon nods.

Dr. Overman consults Keiya's chart, he fills out some forms.

Dr. Overman

Take these to the indicated labs and get the MRI's when you come back we will make a final decision.

Keiya and Mrs. Brandon take the paperwork and leave. Fade:

Keiya and her mother go to a series of blood tests, x-ray labs and for the MRI.

Fade:

Keiya and Mrs. Brandon are back in Dr. Overman's office. Keiya is tense.

The nurse calls them into the office.

Dr. Overman

I have good news for you Keiya. The specialists I have had go over your test results agree with me, the program will be good for you.

I want you to remember to be sure to listen to and adhere to the safety rules. You are going to work with one of our own physical therapists as well as Amber herself.

Can you promise me that if they say it is enough, you will accept that?

Keiya nods.

Dr. Overman

OK, then. I am going to have you come back in at least once a week for awhile. I am going to prescribe three times a week at the ranch, for three hours. Your insurance has agreed to pay for it.

Have a great time.

The doctor extends his hand. Keiya and Mrs. Brandon shake hands and leave.

Fade:

Mrs. Brandon and Keiya drive into the stable. Keiya has riding clothes on, and is pulling her stable shirt on over the top.

Mrs. Brandon help Keiya unload from the van. Bella has come running from somewhere with two other teenage girls. One is in an electric wheelchair.

Bella

Keiya, we have been watching for you.

Come on, we all are going to classes together today.

Bonnie, Adriana, this is Keiya.

The girls greet each other.

Adriana is the girl in the wheelchair.

Adriana

We will be buddies today. Remember what
Bella told you about buddies? We have to
go sign in and stay together all day. We are
responsible for each other.

The girls say good-bye to Mrs. Brandon, and move off
together towards the office.

The girls approach the barns.

Keiya

I am really kind of scared. I am glad Amber
does not let parents in the corral when we ride.
Sometimes my Mom is so scared for me, she
makes me scared.

Adriana

My Mom too. The first class I took here,
she made such a fuss, I thought Amber
would throw us out, but she just got another
Mom, with another child in the same kind of
wheelchair to take her out to the cooking area
for a cup of coffee and a chat.

Bonnie

Even foster parents, my foster Dad brought me
to the first riding class I took. When they told
him he had to stay outside the fence and keep
quiet so the outriders and horses could work

safely I thought he was going to drag me home.
I could see it in his face.

Keiya looks at Bonnie strangely.

Keiya

I don't mean to be rude, or nosy, but why did
you have outriders.

Bonnie

I was in a wheelchair too.

I have a birth defect that causes the muscles to
be too weak and too pain filled to walk. I came
here as a little kid, my physical therapist had
heard horse therapy helped relieve the pain and
help patients with my problems.

It surely did. Now, as long as I keep up
my physical and horse therapy, I do OK.
Sometimes I get tired and have to rest, but it is
OK with me.

Bonnie bounces around the girls in a bouncy dance of delight.
They all laugh and move along the path to the corral.

Inside a copper colored horse, two outriders, and a horse
handler stood chatting with Amber.

There are some helmets hanging by their straps along the
fence. Each of the girls tries on one or two, Bella help Keiya
find one that fits and fastens it.

The Girls

Hi, Penny. Good Penny.

The horse flickers an ear at them, but stands still with her handler.

Amber

Adriana, I wanted you to come and show Keiya
the proper start to her class.

Adriana motors through the gate that Bonnie is holding open for her. She approaches Penny from the side, near her head and stretches her hand out in greeting.

Adriana

Hi Penny. Good Penny.

She rubs the mare's face gently. The horse stands perfectly still as Adriana motors along her shoulder and maneuvers the chair to face the horse. The handler touches the horse on her left lower shoulder. Penny extends her left foreleg, and bends her right into a bow. Adriana picks up her own right leg and swings it up on to the pad. She grabs the vaulting handles and pulls herself on to the horse with the help of the two outriders. She nods, and the horse handler signals Penny, who rises smoothly and stands perfectly still.

Amber

Go ahead and walk her around a couple of
circles. Adriana, do the arm exercises.

Then come over and dismount in front of Keiya
so she can see how to dismount safely.

Adriana, on Penny, is led to her wheelchair. She taps Penny
on the left shoulder, the horse extends her left leg and bows.
Adriana, with the help of the outriders slides backwards until
just her right leg is left on the pad, and she has seated herself
again in the wheelchair. She moves her leg back to the leg rest,
and motors up to Penny's head.

She rubs the mare in small circular motions as she moves
along.

Bella

She is giving her the horsey cookies she
deserves.

Keiya is gently rubbing little circles on her thighs.

Adriana reaches into her pocket and gives Penny a treat from
her flat palm.

Adriana

Thank you Penny. Good Penny.

Bella

Penny loves it when we say Good Penny, and
use her name.

Adriana motors out of the corral as Amber motions Keiya to
come in.

Mr. And Mrs. Brandon have arrived and are standing next to the girls who are removing their helmets.

Keiya waves to them.

Amber

OK Keiya. Let's see what you learned.

Keiya motors up to the front of the horse the same way Adriana had done. She holds her hand out, palm down, and allows Penny to sniff her hand.

Keiya

Hello Penny. Good Penny. Help me, I am new at this.

She moves her left hand along the horse's neck, as she motors back along the horse.

She maneuvers her chair into position facing the pad.

The handler taps Penny's left shoulder and the horse kneels as before. The outrider by her left shoulder helps Keiya to position her right foot on the pad, and her left hand on the vaulting grip on the left. The other outrider helps her to position her right hand on the right vaulting grip and the two assist her in mounting the horse. After she is steady, the horse handler signals Penny, who rises and stands quietly. The outriders help Keiya to settle in the saddle. She is obviously afraid.

Amber

It is all right to be afraid. Just breathe.

Wiggle your arms and shoulders, hang them
loosely. Be like a cloth doll.

Just hang loosely and breath slowly.

Breathe in... .....in........in....

Hold your breath.......

Breathe out.......out........out.

Keiya, head hanging, legs and arms floppy, is breathing in and
out slowly as instructed.

Mr. and Mrs. Brandon are seen, breathing in and out slowly,
hanging on the fence outside the corral.

Amber

OK Keiya, sit up as tall as you can.

I will give you some instructions. We will do
the exercises standing still, then we will ask
Penny to walk.

Remember. I will not ask you to do anything
you are not ready for. If you are not ready, let
me know.

If you need to stop. Say "I need to stop". Do
not scream. Penny does not know that you are
afraid of her. She is an old hand at this, she has
done this job for years. But, she is a horse, and
just knows her rider is afraid. That can make
her afraid, especially if you start screaming.

Do not kick her, and do not wrap your legs around her. That is a signal to go faster. Penny has been here a lot of years and is natural horse trained, but she has been kicked in the past and if you kick her, or wrap around her, she might remember it is a signal to go fast.

Never let your legs below the knee touch the horse. Just let them hang.

Try to grip with your knees.

Keiya begins to do the exercises. Arms over her head, Hands on her knees, Hands on her shoulders. Bending to one side or the other and trying to touch the opposite toes. Stretching as high as she can into the sky.

Amber

Ready?

She motions the horse handler, and the group moves slowly forward. The outriders have their hands on Keiya's knees and Amber walks directly behind the left side outrider and holds Keiya's back steady.

After two circles, Amber begins the exercise commands and Keiya goes through them again.

From time to time Amber says something, and Keiya lets go with one hand and makes the small circular motions on Penny's shoulders.

The group comes to a halt near Keiya's wheelchair.

The horse handler signals Penny to kneel, the outriders and Amber help a Kciya to dismount and get back in to her wheelchair.

Adriana, Bonnie and Bella lead the way with loud applause and cheers. Mr. and Mrs. Brandon join in.

Fade:

The girls are passing through the barns feeding horses carrots.

Mr. and Mrs. Brandon are following along, listening to the chatter as Keiya tells them about each horse, sometimes asking Bella what she has forgotten.

They come to Snow, with his hanging bowl, and special bucket of treats.

Keiya

This is Snow. He has special treats because he is 39 years old. That is like a 135 year old person. But he is Arabian, so that is why he is living much longer than most horses. Some breeds live longer.

Snow still works. He is a favorite for braiding and grooming. He also still does the vaulting program for really small children. Not because he has to work, but because he loves to.

Bella

He is one of the few horses allowed to just roam the ranch. During the hours when there are no students, he can just be turned out to graze, and visit, he loves to visit the other horses.

The people take turns feeding Snow from his bowl, and carrots to the nearby horses who are eagerly looking over, begging.

Fade:

The old horse is following Amber around the ranch. He grabs a bite of the lawn here and there, and looks into the stalls as they pass by other horses. Some of them push their noses out and are eager to touch muzzles with him. Others squeal, and warn him away from their food.

He wanders back to Amber and she absently pats his neck as they walk along checking on things here and there.

Fade:

The group reaches the outdoor cooking area. The chef is finishing up and the students in the front twenty seats are beginning to put huge salads into big bowls on the buffet table. Others are putting plates, silverware, glasses and silverware on the tables.

Several large platters sit by the chef, waiting for the main course to be plated up. The group finds a table and sits. The students come by with large pitchers of iced tea and homemade lemonade. Real lemons and mint are in the pitchers with the ice and lemonade.

Mr. Brandon

Is this a special day?

Amber

No, we have a large number of chefs who volunteer one day every month or so, they choose their menu, and most provide the food for sixty or seventy people.

We eat six days a week.

I like the horses to have a day off, and the staff and volunteers to plan a day for medical appointments, and other scheduled dates. We are closed Wednesday for that purpose. It also gives the maintenance crews time to get their work done without people and horses all over the place.

The lines are forming and the group joins the others at the buffet. Adriana and Keiya join other students in motorized wheelchairs, and regular wheelchairs at a table that is lower to make it easier for them to serve themselves.

Mrs. Brandon

Keiya has become really expert at holding her plate on her lap and serving herself.

Bonnie

It means a lot to not have to rely on someone else for everything.

Mrs. Brandon

Keiya told me you used to be in a wheelchair.

Bonnie

Yes, they had little hope I would ever walk, or be Independent. This program has meant a whole new life for me.

I think the freedom in my mind was the first part.

The biggest part.

One day I was sitting in my wheelchair watching a new horse that had come in……..

Fade:

Bonnie is sitting in a motorized wheelchair, she is not the fun loving girl who had been speaking to Mrs. Brandon. She is younger, and looks deeper than sad.

She is watching two men unload a horse from a trailer. The horse rears up, and thrashes around on the end of his lines. Each of the men hold a line and maneuver the horse into a nearby stall. They shut the door and move away. The horse can be heard kicking the walls and neighing.

After the men leave, Bonnie motors her chair over to the door and peeks in between the cracks of the door and the door jamb.

The horse is beginning to quiet. Finally the horse begins to eat some hay that the men threw on the shavings in the stall.

Amber approaches the stall and opens a small window in the side of the stall. She notices Bonnie watching.

Amber

This was a mustang. Someone bought him, and could not train him. He was beaten by someone who told the owner it was the way to train a horse. To master him. He got so upset, no one could get near him, he was in a round corral and no one could catch him. He was trailing a lead rope and finally he got hungry enough a handler got him for the vet, who tranquilized him, and they brought him here.

The owners still want him, and are hoping we can help them get him to trust us, then them.

I am going to feed him now, then starting tomorrow, he gets food and water only from me. I will feed him for an hour each morning and again after all the students leave. In about four or five days, he will begin to trust me. It is an old Native American way to get horses to trust.

Amber is feeding the horse. One bite at a time, if he acts afraid, or aggressive, Amber takes the food away. Bonnie is watching.

Fade:

Amber is feeding the horse. He is nuzzling her hands, and does not seem to mind as she snaps a line to his halter.

Amber leads the horse, up and down, in his own stall. Bonnie is watching.

Fade:

Bonnie

I watched her train that horse. I watched her gain his confidence.

One day, I just made up my mind, if he could trust her. So could I. And I have.

It changed my whole life.

The group continues to eat, and chat.

Fade:

The group is heading out of the cooking area.

Bella and Bonnie wave, and go towards their riding class.

Adriana and Keiya wave to Mr. and Mrs. Brandon and head for the swimming pool area.

The two girls wheel into the pool area, where they shed their tee shirts and shorts, both are now in swim suits they had on under their clothing.

Adriana

When I first came here, I had to have my Mom put on and take off all of my clothing.

Keiya

I could put on my shirt, but not my shorts, I really liked the class you taught with the swimming teacher to help us all learn how to take off the shorts and put them back on.

I could always put on my socks, but fell over trying to put on my shoes. Thank you for teaching me to put them on and lace them up against a wall.

Adriana

I got so tired of the kids at school making fun of me for not being able to tie my own shoes and having to wait for the gym coach to help me change.

After I came here, I asked the physical therapist to come and talk to my gym class. She is an Olympic Gold Medalist from ten years ago. She brought her medal, and other awards and pictures of all the competitions she had been in.

Fade:

A younger Adriana is sitting in her wheelchair. A group of gym clothing clad girls is sitting around her on the benches in the indoor basketball court. The coach is introducing a young woman.

Coach

This is Beth, she is Adriana's physical therapist. Today she has come to talk to all of us about the sports she competed in and some other things.

The girls are excited about the gold medal, and crowd around Beth as she shows them the scrap book with pictures of her competitions.

                         Beth

     My Mom made this book for me when I was
     about your age.

She pokes a picture in the front of the book.

                         Beth

     All of that competition was exciting, and fun. It
     was also hard other kids made fun of me, and
     said I would never make it.

     Would you have done that?

She looks at each of the girls one by one, they each shake their heads, some look very shamed.

                         Beth

     How about you?

She selects one of the girls who has avoided her eyes, but shook her head no.

                         Beth

     What is your name?

Another Girl

Her name is Courtney, she would have made fun, she makes of all of us, all of the time.

Courtney's face becomes hostile and stubborn.

Beth moves towards her and puts her hand on her shoulder.

Beth

That doesn't feel very good. Talk to me.

Courtney looks at the ground.

Courtney

Yes, I probably would have. And no, it does not feel very good. My Mom and my grandmother constantly tell me how I will never succeed and put me down.

Beth

And how does that relate to your being mean to the other girls? Especially Adriana. She already has enough on her plate.

Courtney surveys the other girls, and stares at Adriana.

Courtney

In after school sports, most of these girls have parents and family who come and cheer for them, talk to them before.

My Mom and Grandmother just tell me all the ways I might make a mistake, and even if I win, they tell me only what I have done wrong.

Courtney is thinking hard. She is also trying not to cry.

Beth

Does making the other girls feel bad really make you feel better?

She gives Courtney a long silent moment.

Courtney shakes her head no.

Coach

How many of the rest of you have the same or similar problems at home? And bring them here to spread on others?

Several of the girls wriggle, but raise their hands. Some of the other girls stare pointedly at others, until they too raise their hands.

Beth

What do you think you could do that would work better?

Xena

With a name like mine, I have had a lot of teasing, then I tease others. I guess I could find some friends who understand and talk to them.

Coach

Yes, maybe we can take time to talk about things for five minutes while we do our warm up stretching. It does not have to be silent.

Beth

That is a great idea.

Sometimes it is hard to tell others they are hurting your feelings, or that someone else has hurt your feelings. But, we can learn to hear someone, and apologize. What would be a reason we might not want to apologize?

Francis

I don't like to apologize because it makes it seem like I am wrong?

The girls giggle.

Francis

Well, I guess I mean, it makes me feel not as good, I know I am wrong, or I would not be apologizing.

At my house, my parents always make us apologize, even if we are not wrong.

Elaine

My parents are like that too. My older sisters pick on me, and when we fight, we all have to apologize to my Mom for bothering HER, or my Dad, when my sisters are the ones being mean to me. No one ever has to apologize to me.

The coach looks at the girls.

Coach

Anyone else have that problem?

Several girls raise their hands, including Adriana.

Coach

Beth came here today to talk about a special kind of bullying. Some of you have been bullying Adriana. I want to know why. I want you to listen to Beth as she explains why Adriana is in that wheelchair.

I want you all to listen carefully, with your hearts.

The girls stop talking as Beth steps forward.

Beth

Adriana is in that wheelchair because someone was driving irresponsibly. She was a little girl, not driving, legally in seat belts and safety approved car chair.

I want to ask each of you if you think you might be next?

Beth looks intensely into the faces of each of the girls present.

Beth

I want those of you who have either bullied Adriana, or another disabled person, to get up and walk up here, shake her hand, shake Keiya's hand, and apologize. Not just to them, but to the others you have bullied because you gave yourself permission to be mean to the disabled.

Beth again looks intensely at each of the girls.

Beth

Do not forget, I know which ones of you have done this. And I know which of you laughed, or did nothing. Get yourselves up and also apologize.

One by one, girls shuffle up, and mumble to Adriana and Keiya.

Beth

Now, every one of you who did not stand up for someone, or Adriana or a small child you saw being bullied......come up here and apologize.

The girls stand confusedly and some have tears on their faces.

Beth

Children are children is NOT an excuse.

Bullying is just normal is NOT an excuse. How many of you want to stand here and let everyone bully you. If it is normal, and so much fun, you would want to by bullied yourself, wouldn't you?

The girls stare at the ground.

Beth

Being disabled, or different in any way, being smaller, or another race, having parents that are not like all the others is not something anyone has control over. YOU have control over being mean.

It is your choice. You are going to look at yourselves and make a commitment to be nicer young women, or you are going to choose to go on being mean bullies.

The girls continue to stare at the ground.

Desiree

I want to apologize for being a mean bully. I thought everyone thought I was funny and laughing.

Andrea

We laughed because we were afraid you would bully us next. We hate you.

Beth

I think you are being honest Andrea, but I also think it takes courage for Desiree to admit she has been wrong for so long.

What can we all do to heal?

The girls buzz with thoughts and suggestions. The coach sets up a dry erase board.

Coach

Let's list some things we can do.

The girls begin to raise their hands....

Fade:

Adriana

That day empowered me to know that I am not less because mean people give themselves permission to treat me like less.

I also learned to ask for help. If I do not get it from one place, keep on asking. If someone says, just let it go, find someone else.

Adriana and Keiya stop talking as an athletic swim instructor strides over to the girls, a couple of other wheelchair swim suited girls are waiting by the heated small therapy pool.

The instructor helps each of the girls out of their chair and into the special handrails that help them maneuver into the pool and sit in a circle around the edges of the pool. When six students are in the pool, the instructor begins to give them exercise instructions, the girls follow along. The instructor turns on a wall switch and music begins to play while the girls exercise.

Fade:

Mrs. Brandon is talking to Amber. They are walking along a pathway towards a small arena that is away from the other riding areas.

Amber

This is our newest program. We have had veterans support programs for a long while. PTSD seems to be a problem that is helped almost immediately in the appropriate type of equine therapy and just plain riding lessons. It all depends on the vet.

We work with the therapists and the vets to establish the right match for each one.

The two have come up to the corral. Around the outside several women are lounging against the bars. Inside the corral a very wild acting horse is stirring up the sand and dirt of the round corral.

A woman, maybe in her mid twenties is concentrated on the freed animal. She has a short rope in her hands and swings it lazily at the horse when it slows. She continues to keep the horse moving, at times stepping in front of the horse and using only the rope, turning the horse and getting it to go the other direction. She never shouts, or hits the horse.

The women around the edges are talking in small groups, or just watching.

Amber

This group is women veterans who have lost their children due to PTSD causing them to abuse their children.

Many of them are so keyed up to sounds in the night, that if a noise wakes them, they have the child slammed up against the wall in a choke hold before they are even really awake.

The children are in another group, you will meet them. Keiya is going to read to them, and volunteer in their art and cooking programs.

Mrs. Brandon

I overheard a young woman talking one day at the lunch table near mine. She said if she could have one wish, it would be to wake up with her kids jumping on her bed, and go out and make pancakes with them.

I thought I would love to volunteer and have a camp out or something that would be similar, and cook pancakes with the women and their children.

Amber

That is a great idea.

Let's have an afternoon campout. We can put out sleeping bags, and the mentors who monitor the visits can come as well.

Fade:

It is a warm afternoon, in one of the round corrals near the cooking area women and children are spreading out sleeping bags, some have air mattresses. They are laughing and joking while they take turns blowing them up.

Everyone is in pajamas and slippers. Some have robes on. A couple have big clown like rollers hanging from their hair, or silly sleep nets on their heads.

Each group is putting out books to read. The Moms and monitoring mentors are getting each family group together. They begin to read, and someone throws a beach ball. The ball bounces and is tossed from here to there.

Fade:

The group is heading towards the cooking area. Large cooking grills have been heated and on the tables are the ingredients for pancakes. Each group takes a pitcher of pancake mix and heads for a portion of the grill. They all make pancakes, some round, some small, some animal or other shapes.

There are bowls of berries, chocolate chips, and small candy that can be sprinkled on the pancakes while they are cooking to make faces.

Everyone is laughing. Some of the pancakes burn, everyone laughs.

Amber is stirring a large amount of sausage and turning even more bacon on a second grill. She piles them into big platters, the women and children grab them.

The groups head for the tables and begin to eat. Fade:

Amber and Mrs. Brandon are watching the woman in the corral. She has stopped moving and turns her back to the horse. The horse slows, and begins to come up to the woman. The woman stands completely still. The horse comes right up to her shoulder and blows her breath into the woman's hair. The woman turns and rubs the horse on the face. She turns and walks away, the horse follows quietly as the woman moves in circles and turns into eight shaped figures. She stops and the horse stands quietly at her shoulder. The woman turns and fastens a halter and lead rope on the horse. She begins to groom the horse with a brush and curry comb.

The group continues to talk or just watch quietly from outside the corral.

The instructor signals the woman, who takes the horse out of the corral. A horse handler releases another horse into the corral. Another young woman bends through the bars and begins the same exercise.

Amber

Some people call this partnering, some call it joining with the horse.

It is based on the horse herd behavior. The horse moves out until it has decided to trust and surrender to the person. In the wild, or even in a field, horses create a working hierarchy for protection. The alpha mares run the herd. The alpha mare will haze another horse until the horse makes the commitment to follow her lead. In the wild this is for herd protection. When the alpha mare sees danger, or the stallion set apart to watch for danger signals danger, often with a flick of ears, the alpha mare will tell the whole herd to move to survive.

The animal that does not pay attention and do what it is told puts the others in danger, and itself at risk of death. Their instinct tells them to give in when they realize they have met a lead mare.

The two women watch as the second veteran goes through the exercise with the new horse.

Mrs. Brandon

How do the horses know when it is time to give in?

Amber

It has a lot to do with the person asking.

Just as the horses know the power of one horse over another, they know the same about people.

A horse may take hours to bother with one person, but join or partner right up with an experienced horse trainer of this type.

On the other hand, a horse that has less instinct and may have been abused, or spoiled by humans may take longer, or even resist the stronger willed person over the less skilled one.

This group of horses have been brought in by a trail riding stable who just bought them. The make a donation and pay for the feed while they are here. The veterans train them to become really reliable trail horses.

Mrs. Brandon

That is wonderful. The reason I am still afraid of horses and was afraid for Keiya to come to this program is because my parents took us on a vacation trail ride.

The horse I was riding just took off running. I got thrown off, I walked back and have never been near a horse again until now.

Amber

It helps not just the horses, it helps the veterans to help someone else. Most stable horses, as long as they stay quiet and calm stay working for years. The older and slower, the better for older and more timid people. It gives the horses a better chance for a good life, having been trained here.

The stables will often sell a horse to a veteran if there is a really good connection. For the most part, those horses stay here and both the horse and the vet are volunteers in our program.

Fade:

Amber is working in a large arena with a group of women and men veterans.

Each of them has a horse on a line, and a saddle, bridle and blanket on the fence near them.

Each of the horse/human couples are doing a warm up exercise.

Amber

Jake, what do we do this exercise for?

Jake

To see what side of the stable the horse got up on.

Amber

Correct. A horse is not a car, or bike. It may, just like a human get up with a headache, or a small injury, or just a grouchy mood.

A lot less riders would get hurt if they evaluate the side of the stable their horse is on before plopping a saddle on the horse and jumping up and kicking and jerking him.

Amber

Annie, what can we evaluate while doing our grooming and warm up exercises?

Annie

You can feel any tender places, find any injuries, and when you start this short line lounge you can see if the horse is limpy or favoring any part that might need attention.

You can hear a lot, or no bowel sounds and check to see if the horse has a stomachache. A horse with severe gas might get forced out to ride and come back, get in the stall and suffer really bad colic.

A horse with a hard, silent tummy might get forced out to ride and drop dead of colic.

Amber

Correct. When you know this, you know enough to even at a rental stable take a quick look at the horse. The horse may have been working part of the day, may have chronic injuries that will not affect the rider or horse. Some older horses are stiff coming out in the morning, but loosen up and are fine later. But, you need to be aware.

Each of the riders expertly and quickly curries and brushes his/her horse, and examines the blanket and saddle for

anything that might cause irritation to the horse. The horses
are quickly saddled and bridled.

Amber

Jake, remind us why we check the blanket,
cinch, and saddle for anything that can irritate
the horse.

Jake

This is called the pre-flight check of the tack.
You might lose your life to an oat, or grass seed
spire under the blanket, cinch, or saddle that
stabs the horse.

Jake picks a piece of oat off the saddle blanket and shoves it
into his palm.

Jake

This hurts. When you thump your body weight
on the saddle and one of these is pointed into
the horse, the most gentle horse might become
a rodeo bunking bronc.

The others nod. Some uncinch their saddles, pull them off and
recheck.

Amber nods in approval.

Amber

I want to remind each of you, that a horse can
feel a fly walking on any part of him. A horse
knows what another horse is saying from long

distances. There is absolutely no excuse for hitting, kicking, jabbing with spurs.

The only real reason for more tack, is lack of human ability to communicate and take control of a horse. Horses are herd animals, used to obeying. They feel safe when someone else is watching out for them. When they partner with you and give you the trust involved in that relationship, you are going to find it easier and easier to be a good partner with your horse.

Mount up.

The riders shake their saddles, some tighten cinches, they mount up and take their places in a circle around Amber.

Amber

Walk.

The riders all move imperceptibly forward, the horses begin to move around the circle in a well behaved class.

From time to time they change gait, or turn around in unison. Ambers directions are barely audible, the horses change gaits and directions smoothly as she directs.

Fade:

Amber and Mrs. Brandon are watching another of the class with a new horse trying to get the partnering or joining exercise complete with a nervous horse that is spewing dirt and sand out of the arena as he spurts forward whenever the vet makes a move.

Amber

This young man is very tense himself. I gave him a very abused and tense horse. He has done this exercise many times with my own personal horses that joins up rapidly.

I expect this exercise to push him out of wherever he had disappeared into. It is impossible to not become completely into the now with the horse, at first because the riders are afraid of horses, and then because, knowing enough, they are attuned to the need for constant attention to keep from getting hurt.

As she speaks, the horse turns and baring its teeth, with ears laid back rushes at the vet in the corral. The vet simply sidesteps him and flaps the air with a long stick with a plastic bag and a bandanna tied on the tip.

Mrs. Brandon looks curiously at Amber.

Amber

I got those sticks long ago in a class I took. They were orange, and called "care sticks". Now many people call them carrot sticks.

The horse has swerved away from the menacing plastic bag and spurted more dirt and sand on the onlookers as he attempts to get away from the vet standing calmly once more in the center of the round corral.

Amber

(laughing)

That horse is right about now saying, that cowboy sure can run. I do not believe a horse really knows that the person is not running right alongside, and as the horse tires, his instincts kick in and tell him to make peace with the alpha horse so he can stop running. The person has not hurt him, so he does not have to stop and fight for his life.

They continue to watch as the horse begins to swivel his inside ear towards the vet, and to slow down.

Amber

He is just about to give this cowboy a chance. He is not looking for a fight. He is not scared. He just does not want to run anymore.

Horses need comfort and companionship, they know that a lone horse is no match for mountain lions, or wolves.

The horse slows, the man stops doing anything and turns his back to the horse. It slows, starts up, and then walks to the man, thrusting its nose towards him from a respectful distance. The man extends his hand, palm down, and lets the horse sniff. Then he rubs the horse on the face, pulls out a halter and lead rope, slips them on and walks away, the lead rope loosely hanging from his hand. The horse follows as he starts to walk here and there and in circles and figure eights.

The man stops from time to time to rub the horse on the shoulder or face.

Amber

One of the old Native trainers I worked with as a teen told me that horses remember that first lick of their mother's tongue to clear the fluids off their face. In the rest of the lives, that smooth, petting gesture is very calming and reassuring to them, it is just hard wired into them.

I have seen horses raised by humans, who even though wiped down with an antiseptic cloth, do not have that same instant reaction to the calm, smooth rubbing on their face.

The two watch with the others as the man, as if only he and the horse exist in the world go through their exercise. No one tells him to hurry, no one interferes.

Amber

This is probably the first time in months either of them has felt safe and not alone.

I personally think that for the vets, the gaining of control over such a large and wild animal, helps them regain a confidence in themselves that has been missing for a long scary time.

I also think that the trust of the animal helps them build a being needed and trusted feeling

that they have gotten too afraid to have maybe
for years and years.

That is just my opinion, the field is all too new
to ask the vets, and the horses aren't talking.

Fade:

Adriana and Keiya are waiting by the van when Mrs. Brandon
walks up with Amber. Keiya loads into the van, more expertly
and more on her own than in previous scenes.

Adriana and Keiya wave goodbye and the van drives off.

Mrs. Brandon does not have the usual loud music on. Keiya is
chattering about all she has seen and done.

Keiya

Mom, you know what? Today we had a class
with the little disabled kids. We helped teach
them how to do some art projects and we read
books with them.

Fade:

Keiya and Adriana are motoring down the path to the library.

Keiya

That was a fun class we had learning how to
read to the little kids.

I had forgotten how much I love some of those
books. Some of the horse books: I am looking
forward to as if they are old friends.

Adriana

Me, too, Misty of Chincoteague Island. The Godolphin Arabian. Margaret Henry.

The Farley books. The Black Stallion. I read the small child version with all the pictures, and the novels. His last book was "How to Stay out of Trouble with your Horse" a non-fiction to help owners stay safe and keep their horses safe.

Keiya

I think it is fun to read to the kids, and see how excited they get about learning new things.

The two girls motor into the library, A small group of young children, some in wheelchairs, some sitting on the carpet clap their hands and shout hello to the two girls.

The girls pick up books and Keiya begins to read. The children, for the most part are quiet and fascinated.

Fade:

Mrs. Brandon and Keiya are in the van continuing on their way home. They stop and pick up Mr. Brandon. Keiya starts the whole story over about the children and reading to them. Mrs. Brandon turns up the radio in the front seat. Dad is sitting in the rear seat near Keiya in her wheelchair.

Keiya

You know what Dad, I really like being able to get the attention of kids who do not know how to listen to a story.

It is kind of like partnering with the horses. When the kids begin to realize they are missing something really fun, and not getting the stickers when I ask questions, they begin to listen.

Mr. Brandon

You are really getting a lot of skills besides horse back riding at the ranch.

I am really proud of how you help others.

Keiya

I do not know if I ever really thought of me having a career.

Now, I think I might want to go to college and get some degrees that will let me work or volunteer with Amber and be even more helpful.

Mr. Brandon

I kept the money for you from that accident in a special account for when you were older. I thought it would be to help you when you get independent to take care of rent and other needs.

Now, I think it is going to be for your education as well.

Keiya

When I first went to the ranch, I just thought of riding a horse like the kids I saw on television.

After meeting Bella, and Adriana, I started to think of more.

And you know what Dad? I think the work I have done at the ranch has helped you somehow too. I used to feel like you felt guilty about the accident, and it was not your fault.

I love you Dad.

Mr. Brandon reaches around his seat and pats Keiya on her arm with a big smile.

Fade:

Keiya, Adriana, Bella, Amber and two horse handlers are standing around a horse.

A volunteer brings up a horse, placing it in a washing rack that has thick sand around the base. One of the horse handlers takes the lead rope and secures the horse to a ring in the front of the wash rack, the volunteer puts a bar in the back.

Amber

I do not like wash racks, and rarely use them.

The only horses that I allow to use this contraption are ones I have personally certified for this work.

The horses for this work are older and calm.

Penny and Snow both have learned to stand with the holding ladder, and do not need the grooming rack.

I have had a horse slip in a wash rack and die from internal injuries. But, for some students who cannot stand alone, the only way they can braid, or groom is with the standing ladder I invented.

Bella, please show Keiya how to use the standing ladder.

Bella holds her hand out to the horse, she runs her hand down its neck, and stands in the waist high contraption. The side bars give her a place to grip, but she can easily reach over and brush the horse.

Amber

Adriana? Your turn.

Adriana motors to the front of the horse, holds out her hand, and motors back, using one hand to touch the horse. She stops, and using the side bars, comes to a standing position. The volunteer holds a bucket of brushes and curry combs for her to select from.

Adriana shows Keiya how to groom the horse, when necessary.

Keiya sits in her chair, and the volunteer slides the ladder to another point on the horses body. Keiya then holds the grips on the ladder and gets back to grooming.

The horse remains quiet and well behaved.

Adriana sits in her chair and one by one goes to each hoof and asks the horse to lift them. The volunteer hands Adriana a hoof pick, then a hoof brush, then the can of hoof oil. She picks, brushes, and oils each hoof.

Amber

> Keiya. I want you to just do as much as you feel you can. You will build strength over time. Your physical therapist feels you are ready for this, so give it a try.

Keiya motors to the front of the horse, holds her hand out for the horse to sniff, and holds one hand on the neck as she motors back to where the ladder is. She lifts herself out of the chair by the grips on the side rails of the ladder, and takes a curry comb and begins to use it on the horse. She sits back in her chair and moves along as Adriana did.

Excited and flushed, she sits back in her chair.

Keiya

> I think I am kind of tired. Can I do this again?

Amber

As many times as you can.

The volunteer opens the back of the wash rack. The horse handler backs the horse out slowly and leads it back towards the barn. Everyone crowds around Keiya with congratulations.

Fade:

Keiya is standing in a ladder. A volunteer is handing her brushes and helping her with the braids on Penny. This time there is no wash rack. Penny stands quietly with her handler. Bella stands by. Keiya expertly goes through the grooming routine. She motions to the horse handler when she wants Penny moved.

Instead of the ladder being moved, Keiya stands in one place as the horse is maneuvered for complete grooming.

Fade:

Keiya is helping Bella put braids in the mane and tail of Penny.

Keiya

This is so much fun. I can hardly wait to see the children's faces when they see Penny with all her ribbons and flowers and feathers.

The girls finish up with the horse and Bella leads her, Keiya motoring along in front to a round corral that is covered, with a small stadium seating section along one side.

The seating area is filled with small children. Some are a little rambunctious, some are in wheelchairs, others in motorized wheelchairs. Some have walkers, or canes.

As soon as one sees Penny, a scream is heard, all the kids look, and they all begin to scream and shout.

Bella holds up her hand, and most of the noise stops. Bella and Keiya enter the round corral with Penny.

A pair of horse handlers takes the lead rope from Bella and quickly and expertly flip a brush over the horse, clean out her feet and put her pad and vaulting circingle on. One of the handlers stands to the side, the other holds Penny quietly in the middle of the corral.

The out riders arrive and begin, with Bella and Keiya's help, to line up the small children for their turn riding on Penny.

Keiya watches the first child enter, and go through the initial hello and mounting routine.

Keiya

(to one of the children near her)

You have ridden before. That was a really good hello and mounting performance.

Barry

Wait until you see me.

The little boy stands as close to Keiya's chair as he can get, stretches up and stares her eye to eye. Keiya laughs and claps her hands in joy. The little boy laughs, and rushes back to his place in line.

Keiya continues to watch as the line of children go up, mount, do a few exercises, have their picture taken, get stickers on their shirt for all the things they did right without reminding, and as the last one dismounts looks at the horse handler.

Keiya

Would it be OK if I just say thank you to Penny. I have really missed working with her since I moved on the the next class.

It was so nice to help braid her mane and tail and put in the ribbons and all.

The horse handler moves closer and waited for Keiya to thank the little mare and give her a mint.

Fade:

Keiya is sitting at the dinner table, with Mr. and Mrs. Brandon Mr. Brandon is opening a large red envelope. It is made of construction paper, and is decorated by childish drawings of horses.

Mr. Brandon

(reading the invitation)

You are invited to attend.......

Well Keiya, your first horseshow off the ranch.

I am so proud, and excited.

Keiya

We have been helping the little kids all week with their performance.

Amber says they are the ones the newscasters like to put on the evening news.

So, we have had some of the older foster kids taking video tape and making a little CD for them to each have one. They are all now experts at being interviewed for television.

There are so many parts of the ranch that no one sees though.

Mr. Brandon

Tell me.

Fade:

Amber is walking on the trail with a group of children, they are a stair step of ages and sizes. Amber has one horse, and a small child is riding the horse. Amber is leading the horse.

As they walk along, Amber selects a child randomly and the children change places.

Fade:

Keiya

Amber has programs for children who do not get along or mind at home, or at school.

She has whole families who come to ride. When they first come they fight, and hit each other and push to be first all the time.

When she takes them on trail rides, they have learned in the round corral that she is the boss, and they have to follow her directions. It is almost like the horses. She never yells at them, just keeps working, working, working, and one day they all are really well behaved and caring together.

Fade:

Amber is outside a large school. She is standing near the school bus stop. A long line of busses is waiting. A bell sounds, and children pour out of the buildings and run towards cars waiting down the street, and to the busses.

There is a lot of pushing and shoving.

Amber walks along the rows. She takes a child, here and there by the hand and leads them to the end of the line, she motions for them to sit down, facing away from the busses.

Fade:

Keiya

Amber does work for schools to help big groups of students learn to behave better.

She says that when she makes the ones who push to the front go and sit backwards in the rear until the busses are loaded up, and then leads those sitting and chooses a seat for them, it is only about two or three days before the students all develop better bus manners. Mr. and Mrs. Brandon and Keiya continue their dinner.

Mr. Brandon

It sounds as if Amber uses the same strategy on the students as she does on horses.

Keiya

Amber says that too. She says that children and teens are not ready to be the boss, and it makes them too nervous to be in charge.

I thought that was a strange way to look at spoiled, pushy kids but Amber says their parents probably do not know how to help their children be better citizens. Just like horses. Horses live in herds and need to be good citizens for their own safety as well as the safety of others.

The Brandons nod.

Fade:

Mr. and Mrs. Brandon are preparing for bed.

Mr. Brandon

I thought, when you took Keiya to riding lessons, it would be a diversion for our little special girl.

I think it has been a life lesson for me about not keeping our daughter from being all that she can be.

I never expected anything from her, I realize now.

Mrs. Brandon

In the parents class, I learned that I just tried to make up to her for all she did not have. I tried too hard to protect her from anything that might further hurt her.

I learned that I was keeping her from being all that she can be, by not letting her be her own personal best. Any child can and will get injured, but when I was teaching the class with the parents of gang member…

Fade:

Mrs. Brandon is at the front of the library. She is reading from a computerized power point display on a large screen in the front of the room.

A group of parents is sitting at the tables.

Mrs. Brandon

I know most of you are here because the Court mandated you to come.

Most of you have a child who is coming out of jail soon.

What are you planning when you pick up your child.

Voices sound out answers.

Parent One

My Mom is having a special family dinner, we missed my daughter.

Parent Two

We are going to his favorite restaurant, then to buy him some clothes. He really hated those clothes in jail.

Parent Three

I'm taking my son to his friend's house. Their family invited us over for dinner.

Parent Four

We are taking the family out for dinner, I hate to think of the awful food they made my daughter eat in jail.

Parent Five

Oh, me too. I got all my son's favorites.

Parent Six

(Others are murmuring similar scenarios) I am with the favorite restaurant parents.

Amber

(who has entered the room)

We have a special guest.

One of the Judges who teaches the Parent Project.

Judge Bertrando?

This is Judge Bertrando, a certified Parent Project trainer for the parents, and the youths.

Judge Bertrando takes the microphone from Mrs. Brandon.

Judge Bertrando

I want each of you to think seriously on each of these Issues.

Your child has put him or herself in serious risk of harm by getting put in lock down. Your child has put your family at risk by their friendships with criminals.

There are many crimes in which family members have been injured or killed because of the misbehavior of brothers, sisters, sons, daughters, nieces, nephews grandchildren.

Your child has shamed you as parents, and shamed your family.

And yet each of you has sat here and told us that you intend to reward your child for that bad behavior.

A rumble goes around the room as the parents talk about the judge's words.

Judge Bertrando

Five days a week I see your child, in one form or another.

Children and teens who have given themselves permission to put the whole family at risk with their bad behavior.

I want to hear some of the reasons you have not turned your child around before this point.

Before you begin, I want you to hear some of the excuses

I hear in Court....

Fade:

Judge Bertrando is seated in his Court. A teen is standing in the docket.

Judge Bertrando

To be eligible for this program, you have to start by telling me exactly why you are here.

Teen

My friend Joe and I went to his Dad's house,
He said his Dad needed us to take the radio out
of the car and bring it down to the shop to be
fixed.

Judge Bertrando stares silently at the teen.

The teen stirs uncomfortably and looks to the lawyer for
guidance. The lawyer stares at the floor.

Judge Bertrando

And that's your story? Where is the Dad?
Where is Joe?

He peers out into the Court. No one stirs.

Judge Bertrando

So, you expect me to believe you are so
incapable of figuring out a situation that you
believed that story?

The teen stares at this lawyer, then his parents. The silence
deepens.

Judge Bertrando

How do you expect to get anything from a
diversion program if you cannot even figure
this out.

Judge Bertrando motions to the clerk.

The clerk starts an overhead projector, a huge picture of a destroyed vehicle is shown on the screen on one wall.

Judge Bertrando

Well?

The silence is harsh.

Judge Bertrando

You need to answer me, or I will give you a week in jail to figure out your answer.

Teen

He told me his Dad had lost the key, and we had to get that radio to the shop.

Both parents stare at the floor.

The Judge keeps staring at the teen.

Teen

I mean, it was his Dad's car, and we had to break in.

The people in the Court laugh, the Judge pounds his gavel.

Judge Bertrando

I am going to order you to jail for a week to figure out if you are sure that is the truth. When you come back we will make a decision on where you are going.

Do you understand that I can decide to put you in to adult court?

Teen

(barely audible) OK sir.

I do remember. We broke into the car after we saw the lady with the little kids and a baby in a stroller go into the fast food place.

Joe told me……..

The glare the Judge gives the teen is almost audible.

Teen

We just wanted to get some fast money. We wanted to buy some video games.

The parents continue to stare at the floor.

Judge Bertrando

I am going to order you into this program. You will spend six months in a lock down treatment program for "video games".

You…..

The Judge motions at the parents.

Judge Bertrando

You will go to a special parenting program, I teach the class, you are not allowed to be late, or miss a class.

There is no excuse.

If you are late, you will make up the class. If you miss a class, you will start over.

The classes are once a week, for three hours, ten weeks.

When you have finished the class, you will start a class with each of your children, one at a time.

I do not expect to see any more of your children, or this one, in trouble again.

The parents confer briefly with the lawyer.

Lawyer

Agreed. The parents would like to know more about the diversion.

Judge Bertrando

This diversion program is until your child reaches the age of 25. During the next six months we will work on a contract. Each juvenile makes up their own contract.

IF, at the age of 25 all terms of the contract have been met, the whole file goes away. The matter dismissed and cleared.

IF, at any point the contract is not met, your child will, upon agreement in the contract, with a signature from each of you and your lawyer, be convicted as an adult of this crime and serve the maximum. The incarceration will be in a juvenile mental lockdown, which all juveniles visit prior to signing the agreement until age 18, then transfer to an adult jail or prison depending on the time left to be served.

One of the terms is that the juvenile work and pay back the damage done. In this case the insurance company has paid, every penny will be paid back to that company before the contract is finalized and dismissed.

You agree to the parenting program. And to the terms of that program as you learn how it works.

The parents discuss with their lawyer again.

Lawyer

Agreed.

The parents leave the Court with their lawyer, the teen is taken out, still in handcuffs with a chain held by the bailiff.

Clerk

Andrew Merck.

Another bailiff leads a teenage boy forward. He too is handcuffed and shackled to a thick chain.

The bailiff chains this teen to iron rings in the docket.

A somewhat disheveled woman dressed more for a night club than a Court stands up and starts to move towards the boy.

Judge Bertrando

Sit down Madam.

The woman glares at the Judge and the bailiff, but sits on the edge of the chair.

Judge Bertrando

OK, Andrew, your turn. Why are you here, start at the beginning.

Andrew

I was sick, the p.....I mean co.......I mean police arrested me.

Judge Bertrando shuffles through the thick file before him.

Judge Bertrando

I see here you were told if you missed one day of school, you would be arrested on a prior crime.

You were stealing things in the super market?

Before the Judge can complete his sentence the Mother has jumped up and started to rave.

Mrs. Merck

You are just trying to gang up on Andrew, he was sick.

You…..

Judge Bertrando

I suggest Mrs. Merck, that you sit down, or you are going to spend some time in jail. NOT with Andrew.

I am beginning to get a very clear picture of what is wrong with Andrew.

The woman begins to bluster again, the bailiff moves towards her. She quiets.

Judge Bertrando

Your son was not sick that day. His social worker was shopping in that store he robbed. The term is robbed. He took things handed to him by others, and ran out the door with them. He handed them to others outside.

His social worker told the store who he was, and reported back to the court. That is his job.

You lied. You knew he was not home, and that he was not sick.

Now you think you can come into my Court and continue The lies, scenes and tantrums documented in your sons file. I am going to give you one chance.

You learn how to dress for a class, and you come to the parenting class. I am restricting you. You will not be allowed to visit Andrew the entire six months he is in the lock down treatment program.

IF you miss one class, or are one minute late, I will know just how much you "love" Andrew.

You are going to agree to see a psychiatrist and the only way you will legally see Andrew again is when the psychiatrist signs you as appropriate to parent a troubled teen.

Do we understand one another madam?

The woman nods. She is angry, but looks at the bailiff and moves out of the Court.

Judge Bertrando

Now Andrew, try again.

Fade:

The parents are stirring and mumbling among themselves.

Judge Bertrando

It is time to get your children in order. We are going to go watch some abused rescue horses sent here for retraining.

As you watch the process. Think of your own child. The abuse may have been gangs, and bullies that caused your child to make wrong choices to feel safe.

The problems may be divorces, death in the family, illness in the home. But, like these broken hearted horses, we are going to partner up with them for their own best lives.

The group follows Amber and the Judge out the door to one of the corrals where a group is partner exercising one horse after another.

The parents go to another corral and one after another try partnering with horses who are already trusted and skilled at partner exercises.

The group returns to the library.

Judge Bertrando

What did you learn out there? What are you going to do now when your child comes home?

Hands raise.

Fade:

Keiya and Adriana are motoring towards the cooking area.

Keiya

I've never met real criminals before. The reading class we did with them was scary for me, now they just seem like friends.

Adriana

And a lot of them have never met a really disabled rider before.

The two girls laugh and enter the cooking area where a group of young people are seated at the tables. Two armed bailiffs are in attendance.

Keiya looks at the guards, and then at Adriana. Adriana just motions her forward.

The youths notice them and wave or smile.

Bella and Bonnie are at the front of the group explaining the cooking lesson.

Bonnie

Here come our other two cooking professors.

The youths look around, and then realize she is talking about Keiya and Adriana.

Bonnie

Keiya, Adriana. Everyone is going to make a name tag so introduce yourselves while helping.

Bella has asked a young man at the nearest table to help her. The two rapidly pass out big bowls, and measuring spoons and measuring cups.

Keiya and Adriana pass out nametags and wait for each young person to make a nametag and put it on their shirt. All are wearing the stable logo shirts.

Bonnie

(pointing)

Here, are the ingredients.

We are going to make cowboy bread on the grill. We have jam, peanut butter and we are going to make butter.

Please remember if you are allergic to milk, or peanuts, or wheat.

Raise your hands if you have allergies.

No hands are raised.

Amber and Mrs. Brandon walk down the path and come into the cooking area.

Mrs. Brandon is watching her daughter moving rapidly in her chair, here and there helping youths at different table with their recipes.

Mrs. Brandon

I had no idea when I brought Keiya here what she would learn and accomplish.

To actually sit here and watch her teaching others. I would never have dreamed when I said yes to riding.

Amber

No one knows what we really do here. Most people think we have little kids with brain injuries or birth defects riding around in circles.

I have had many people come and demand to know why their family member has not learned to ride a horse. They have no idea that riding is not the end goal here. Balance and healing are the goals.

There was one young girl who came, she was so afraid. The first day she would not come in the front gate. I got her a buddy, and we all sat outside the gate talking.

Time after time she came, each time moving a little closer with her buddy. She finally would watch her buddy groom a horse and ride, but from outside the corral.

She listened as we taught class after class of riders how to deal with fear. One day, she just said she was ready and came into the corral with me and her outriders. All she did was the hello horse part. She was doing all the breathing exercises for riding, but she was just standing next to an old horse.

While Amber is talking, the youths have gotten up, one at a time with their recipe cards and bowls and gone along the table with Keiya, or Adriana, or one of the other youth teachers for the day. They have measured out their ingredients and gone back to their tables.

While one group is measuring flour out of the big bag into their bowls, a little wind blows through the cooking area. Flour rises up out of the bowls and covers everyone. Some of the youths start to get mad, but then laugh with the rest.

Chef

Guess we got a little snowstorm today.

The tension eases and all the youths laugh at themselves and each other, covered with flour.

Amber

Two weeks ago, these kids would have beaten up each other and anyone else out here just because the wind blew a little flour on them. Their work in their anger management class and with the parenting program is helping.

Mrs. Brandon

I think being protective of the disabled children helps them as well. I watched one day, I have to admit I was very afraid for Keiya to be with criminals.

I was watching in the reading class, I saw all but one of the teens change from scared, fighting horse to partnering student with the others. I guess I mean scared, fighting teen...

Amber

You are not the only one who says horse when I mean child, or even adult.

You yourself even admitted you are glad of the growth for Keiya. Yet when you first came, if I had suggested that she would be teaching a cooking lesson to gang members, you would have run away down the road.

Mrs. Brandon nods, and the two turn back to watching the youths stir and knead their cowboy bread, put it on sticks, and one by one find a place on the large grill and cook the bread slowly, turning it over and over.

As the bread is finished, the group is passing around a big bowl with a hand mixer in it. Each one takes a turn. Finally the Chef look in the bowl.

Chef

Just a few more people. Keep beating. The butter is now about to form

A couple more teens take a turn whipping the cream and suddenly the butter begins to form, and in a moment, the butter is in a couple of balls in a bowl of watery milk.

Chef

This is called buttermilk. We will save it for the pancake mix.

The chef shows one of the teens how to push the butter together with a wooden spoon, and pour off the buttermilk into a storage container. Bonnie takes the container inside to the refrigerator.

The chef gently washes the butter in ice water from a pitcher and molds it into a few shapes, which he places on the table with the jam, peanut butter and napkins.

Chef

Let's eat.

The hungry teens spread butter, jam and peanut butter on their bread, held in their hands in a napkin

Amber pats Mrs. Brandon on the back and moves to the front of the class.

Amber

This bread can be made from frozen dough, prepared dry biscuit mix, or bread and rolls in cans. Just be sure if you make it at home you have an adult to\ help you with the stove or fire, if you make it outdoors.

You can make the bread in the oven or even in a dutch oven.

Amber shows them a dutch oven.

Amber

This oven can be set inside a regular oven, it can be placed in the barbeque. On the beach or in a campsite, it can be placed in the cools after they have stopped flaming and are settled, or on rocks that rest on top of the settled coals.

I need to tell you, it takes a long time to learn how to cook good bread in a dutch oven. I made a lot of burnt, yet gooey in the middle bread before I got the idea. I still can make mistakes and ruin my bread.

Tell me something about cowboys.

The kids raise their hands.

First Teen

Cowboys are rich, they have cows, they own horses.

Second Teen

Cowboys get all the girls.

The kids laugh.

Third Teen

Cowboys carry guns.

Second Teen

Then you must think you a cowboy.

The kids laugh, but stop when Amber starts talking.

Amber

The original cowboys were. BOYS. As time went along Girls cut their hair, and hid the fact that they were girls.

The original cowboys were mostly orphans, maybe ten, or eleven years old. They would get to have a horse to ride, had to ride bareback until they saved enough salary to buy a saddle.

They rode in rags, and often barefooted until they saved enough to buy boots.

Often the cowboys got food, and a place to sleep when they were not out on the range guarding the cattle. When the cattle were driven in to market, they got paid. Sometimes they got nothing,\ the ranchers either did not get enough for the cattle to pay them, or ran off with the money without paying them.

The teens grumble.

Teen Four

That ain't right. If the cowboys worked, they should get paid.

Amber

That is true, but even today, all over the world, people trick others to make them work for free.

The cowboys worked hard, riding for hours and watching the cattle, bringing them together for long cattle drives when area ranchers took the cattle to the nearest train loading areas for sale and shipment to the cities.

Teen One

What about school?

Amber

There was no school for poor children. Rich children had tutors at home, or were sent away to boarding schools.

Teen Three

How come no one taught us this at school?

Amber

Cowboys are probably not an important topic for school.

I learned about cowboys in a PhD program on business. The Professor was teaching us how small businesses started in America by very young people. Many young girls came to America as servants to rich women and their daughters. They had been sewing and taking care of clothes since they were five or six years old.

Many of these young girls would run away and go to work for a clothing factory, or a salon for rich women in another city. Many of the salons were owned by women who had started small sewing businesses in their rented rooms after they got home from work.

The girls were saving money, and hope chests of china, linen and other household items and married cowboys who saved enough money to buy their own farm or ranch.

A few dairy cows, goats, and chickens could create a good business for a young couple.

Mrs. Brandon listens, fascinated.

The young people are enjoying their bread and soon are finished.

                    Amber

How do you guess cowboys washed their dishes? The teens raise their hands.

                   Teen Five

        With water?

The others laugh.

                    Amber

Good guess. But in some desert areas the only water was the water the cattle were drinking. In those areas, the cowboys cleaned their dishes and pans with sand, and plants.

They had to learn the plants early. A wrong plant could easily poison them.

Amber points to a bush growing in a plant behind the cooking area.

Amber

This plant was commonly called "cowboy cologne". Can anyone guess why?

A murmur goes around the group.

Mrs. Brandon shyly raises her hand.

Amber

Mrs. Brandon?

Mrs. Brandon

Because it smelled nice and they could not afford cologne?

Amber

Close. It was called cowboy cologne because water was often scarce, and the cattle will not drink disturbed or dirty water, so cowboys could not bathe in the drinking holes for the cows.

So, when they went into town, or had a dinner date at some boarding house for young women, or were going to a social at a church, they rubbed this plant all over instead of taking a bath.

They rubbed it on their hair to cover the smell of unwashed hair.

Once in awhile the "cookie" or chef, would find a good source of water and boil up big buckets full to fill the old tubs they kept on the cooking wagon out on the range. The cowboys would have a bath. They had to share the water, one after another. The "cookie" often had cooked up some harsh range soap out of fat left from cooking meat, and plants he knew how to use to scent the soap, one was cowboy cologne.

When everyone was through bathing, they all had a turn at washing out their clothes.

On rainy days, everyone brought out their dirty clothes, they didn't have many, just a couple of work shirts, a Sunday go to meeting shirt, a pair or two of jeans, and a pair of boots if they were lucky. Socks were a luxury. Socks were something young women made for their "man".

These young boys knew how to sew, and patched up their own clothes while out on the range.

The young people have started washing their dishes in warm soapy water, rinsing it in the outdoor sink on the cook stand.

The hot water steams away. Those who are finished are washing the tables off and raking the ground around the tables.

Fade:

Mr. and Mrs. Brandon and Keiya are in the van.

Mr. Brandon

I am looking forward to this dress rehearsal of your students. I am proud of you Keiya. You have done a lot of work on these.

He pats a large pile of costumes in a box on the seat.

Keiya

When they told me there were lions and tigers and bears in the horseshow, I wondered.

There have been a lot of surprises in this program. I started out thinking it would just be private riding lessons. I had no idea.

Fade:

Keiya, Adriana, Bonnie, Bella and several others, boys and girls, in wheelchairs and not, are in the library looking at a box of costumes. A group of small children are sitting at the tables, looking at the costumes with joy. They are making a lot of noise in their excitement.

An older woman, with an apron, measuring tape, a hanging pin cushion on her shoulder, sits at a sewing machine.

Helda

Let's get going. Each of you, find a younger partner.

She looks at the older youths.

Helda

I am going to bring out one costume at a time, try and help your partner to choose one that they want.

Let's write down the choices. First, Second, Third choice.

Then we are going to give every team a number.

The teams discuss and write on the little papers handed out by Bella. Helda gives Adriana some numbered papers to hand out.

The process begins.

Soon each of the small children is in a costume of his/her choice.

Helda

I am going to call the numbers again. Each team come up so I can mark the costume for repair.

Fade:

Mr. and Mrs. Brandon and Keiya have arrived at the ranch and unload Keiya. The three head for the library. A loud sound comes out. As they enter, they are greeted by a group of romping lions and tigers and bears.

One of them separates from the crowd and shrieking Keiya's name runs over and hugs her knees and stands on her foot rests to reach up and look right in her eyes.

Child

I bet you do not know who this is.

Keiya

You are right, I just see the most fierce bear.

Watch out Mom and Dad, this bear might not
be friendly.

Mr. and Mrs. Brandon jump backwards in mock fear. The little bear bursts out laughing and runs back to the romping crowd of costumed animals. Soon the whole group is growling and snarling and slapping their paws in the air at the two adults and Keiya.

Keiya motors around in mock fear and finally lets the group of animals catch her. The little animals crowd around hugging and growling and snarling all the while laughing.

Fade:

Mr. and Mrs. Brandon are sitting in the stands with other parents, and family members.

A big tractor with a long attachment smoothes out the arena.

Mr. Brandon

I feel as nervous as if she was riding a bucking
bronc in the rodeo.

Not just a dependable favorite from the school.

He is shouting because of the noise of the machine.

Other parents laugh and nod.

Announcer

Ladies and Gentlemen:

The Grand Entry: Veterans, and our students are going to bring in the flag of our nation. We will all rise while a group of the students sing the national anthem.

Then we will all say the Pledge of Allegiance. And on with the show.

The gates open and a rush of riders on horses of all descriptions gallops into the arena, sweeping around the edges. Most of the riders carry flags. The first two are huge American Flags. Many of the other flags are hand drawn, some obviously drawn by small children.

The crowd rises to its feet.

On both sides of the announcer's booth, students rise and begin to sing the National Anthem.

From the tiniest wheelchair bound students to some very tall veterans and teens the crowd is filled with singing, smiling faces.

As the song ends, the announcer begins to say the Pledge of Allegiance. The riders in the Grand Entry stop and salute the giant flags held by the two leaders who have moved to the center of the arena and stopped.

As the Pledge of Allegiance ends, the horses leap back into motion and gallop around another time and then out of the arena, the crowd erupts into applause and cheering. The two riders with the huge flags gallop around the arena and exit.

The Announcer

Our first performers of the day are the youngest.

The tiny children in their wheelchairs are each accompanied by a teen. Some are recognizable from the cooking class for the gang abatement class. The children and the teens are all dressed in jeans, boots, white tuxedo shirts and sleeveless jeans jackets with their awards on them. They all wear formal bow ties, correctly tied.

The teens push the wheelchairs, or jog beside the motorized wheelchairs filled with lions, tiger and bears.

The horses, each with three rodeo clowns in attendance walk into the arena. The music starts: Animal crackers in my soup.

The tiny children move with their teen escort to their assigned horse. The clowns (horse handlers) have lined the horses up in a straight line. As the children move up the other two clowns in each group stand on each side until the horse handlers asks the horses to kneel. The crowd gasps as the horses kneel in unison and the tiny riders mount. The teens take the wheelchairs out of the arena.

The horse handlers signal and the horses rise as one. The crowd bursts into applause.

The lions and tigers and bears do their exercise and vaulting routines. At the end of the music, the horses are again lined up in the middle of the arena. The names of each horse is called, teens rush out and fasten big show ribbons on each bridle. The horses bow their heads in unison as the last ribbon is given. The audience cheers and applauds loudly.

The announcer then calls the names of each of the lions and tigers and bears. The teens rush out and give each one a trophy, a picture is taken.

The horse handlers, and outriders jog around the arena with their small charges still sitting on the vaulting pads. The children hold up their trophies, smiling at all the applause and cheers.

The horses are again lined up and the teens return with the wheelchairs. The outriders help their tiny charges into them, and amid applause and snapping camera lights they exit the arena holding their trophies high.

Keiya is in her chair, sitting next to Adriana. Bella is in front of them on a chair.

Keiya

I don't think any of them realizes that everyone got a trophy.

Adriana

I don't think they would care. They are so happy to be applauded and cheered for. Most of these kids have been bullied and made fun of or stared at in stores and restaurants in negative ways all their lives.

Bella

I remember my first trophy. I thought I had won the Olympics I was so excited. Amber says that in some things everyone is a winner. These little kids are a miracle to begin with. Most of them have diagnosis for short lives from their medical problems. But they are so cheerful and love everyone so much.

When I teach them in reading or cooking class they call me teacher, or big girl, and they always want to hug me and tell me thank you.

On my worst days, they make me realize my problems are small compared to theirs. Many of them are not just disabled, they were abandoned by their birth families. Some have found foster homes, a few are adopted, but most live in group homes.

The girls watch as the next group of riders enters the arena. This is a group that can ride alone, but need help to mount.

Keiya waves to a little boy who waves at her from his wheelchair.

Keiya

YAY, Tony!

The little boy smiles bravely at Keiya.

The children enter with teens helping them and mount their horses. The horse handlers and outriders are all dressed like cowboys and cowgirls from the old west.

This group has saddles and as their outriders get them settled, each child takes the reins and moves his or her horse towards the outer rail of the arena. The children begin to walk, then trot, then canter in patterns to the applause of the audience. The outriders jog along the rail with their child and horse.

Flashes from cameras, cheers and applause follow their routine. The music ends and the children line their horses up in the center. The horse handlers snap on the lines, the horses and children all bow their heads to the audience. More applause and cheering breaks out.

This group also is announced, one horse at a time, one child at a time and awarded ribbons and trophies. The whole group walks around the arena, the children holding up their trophies and they exit amid applause and cheering.

Keiya leans over the rail, Bella holds on to her chair, she is tipped so far over the edge.

Keiya

Way to go Tony.

The little boy beams as he passes by Keiya.

Adriana

YAY, Tony.

The two girls continue to cheer the little boy and wave as he leaves the arena.

Announcer

Our next group is the ribbon team racing competition

A group of riders enters the arena and canters around the arena. They line up along one side of the arena in pairs.

Each of the teams is given a ribbon. The music starts, and the teams begin exercises that start at a walk, and are simple, the music gets faster, the exercises increase in speed, and complexity. One by one the teams drop their ribbon and line up along the edge of the arena.

Finally, one team is left. The music is fast, the horses are cantering in complex exercises. The crowd cheers and applauds. The music and the two riders stop.

The announcer calls the names of the horses, who each receive a ribbon. Then the announcer begins to call the names of the riders, from the last to the first, each one receives a ribbon. The last team gets a trophy for both of the team members.

The group sweeps around the arena once more, and exits with loud applause and cheering.

Older riders come in to the arena one by one. The announcer tells a little about each group.

Announcer

We have come to the exhibition part of our
show. Each of these riders has created their
own individual exhibition riding experience to
share.

One by one, riders in costumes, or dressed as cowboys,
cowgirls, or in performance Spanish riding costumes, English,
or western performance riding clothes come in and perform
for the crowd.

Announcer

Our next performer is Keiya Brandon.

Keiya motors into the arena, accompanied by a teen, who
jogs next to her. Bella brings a white mare into the arena.
The horse is decorated with ribbons, flowers and feathers and
beads on long leather strings. The horse is wearing a saddle
covered with a beautiful cover with Native American pictures
painted by Keiya during art classes.

Announcer

Keiya painted the saddle cover for her ride
herself.

She also braided and decorated her horse.

Her horse handler just got her certification.
This is her first show as a horse handler.

Bella touches the horse, who kneels, and the outriders assist
Keiya to transfer from the chair to the saddle. The teen takes
her chair to the end of the arena.

Bella touches the mare, and she rises. The crowd applauds. The music starts. Keiya and the mare start the long walk around the arena, the outriders walk beside her, but she has the reins herself. The music speed increases, and Keiya moves the horse to a trot.

The crowd applauds.

Keiya is circling the arena. The horse turns into the carousel horse seen in the first scene, this time Keiya is riding it as the tiny music box turns.

THE END

About the Author

The author is the Training Director for National Homes for Heroes/Spirit Horse II equine therapeutic and healing riding programs. She developed EquiTherapy©™ and AquaTherapy©™ for her clients. These programs are taught with the therapists for the riders, and/or the doctors and physical therapists for the riders.

Many of the riders are there just to ride. They are able bodied, and have had incredible terrors to overcome in their lives. Healing riding is described as being with your horse.

The author has many horse owners who donate their time, and their animals to the programs so that should there be an emergency, there will not be a large number of animals without a place to be, or be cared for.

A Native American, the author was the first of her nation's women to complete law school. A high fever disease caused brain injuries that caused eight years to pass for her to be able to walk and talk well enough to walk hot horses for her younger son who was becoming a horse trainer. Volunteering in equine therapy programs, and in programs with psychiatrists and psychologists who worked with high risk kids, she combined the two, with great results.

Following a shut down due to cancer, the programs are now being restarted. The author is a member of Horses4heroes a national network of horse facilities that donate time to veterans and their families for a ride to help them heal and find a place of peace horsemen know is on a horse.

This book is donated to National Homes for Heroes/Spirit Horse II to raise funds for housing and new therapeutic riding programs for veterans and high risk youths.

DISCLAIMER: This book is completely fiction, but is based on a mix of many of the stories of the author and those she has heard, over the years in this work.

The children's story is an inclusive story, written for each child to be allowed to draw pictures, and discuss with teacher, or parent and other students what the words mean. Drawing pictures allows the reader to engage more completely in the story written.

The screenplay was written for a Producer who wanted to make a movie about equine therapy as his child had loved it. However, he was no longer producing when the book was completed, so the author is looking for a production group to make this movie to give the viewers a complete picture of therapeutic horsemanship.

Spirit Horse II-Certification of Animals and Humans in program

Spirit Horse II warns everyone: Do NOT rely on movies and television shows about horses. Horses are huge wild animals. One bee sting, or bad injury or illness can turn the sweetest horse into a dangerous half ton of danger for humans. DO NOT ever forget that a horse is a horse, not a human or a pet. Learn the horse safety rules and obey them for the safety of everyone and the animals. Those feet are covered in either aluminum or steel, have respect for them. Do NOT ever walk behind horses, let horses know you are approaching, do NOT startle them. They kick when defending themselves.

Animals certified in Spirit Horse II are trained using the Delta Animal Certification videos and training manuals. The animals for Delta Certification are going to be working with severely disabled or hospitalized children and adults. The animals working in Spirit Horse II are working with active, and often high risk clients. The need for our own certification process led us to develop our own criteria, for certification, but Delta is a wonderful and humane system for training therapy animals, or pets, we encourage anyone to use their website to purchase and complete their online or in person courses.

Spirit Horse II is also dedicated to the ideal that all of our animals are our partners in a business created to help heal others. Whether human or animal. Therefore, once an animal is accepted into Spirit Horse II, it cannot be sold and must be provided care for life. Spirit Horse II does not ask our volunteers to stop volunteering as they age or become disabled. An ear, an audience for class, extra eyes to watch everyone for safety are always welcome.

The major difference between certifications for Delta and Spirit Horse II is the need for Delta animals to be quieter, and score higher on skills assessment certification testing. A Spirit Horse animal may be old, disabled, or not able to perform regulatory testing to the standard of Delta, but still is well able to perform safely and in good health for Spirit Horse II members.

For example: A young, bouncy dog that is not able to pass the rigorous sit and stay tests for Delta Certification may be just what Spirit Horse II needs for young students who are very well able to deal safely with a dog bouncing and jumping around them. In a Delta program, the same dog would be unsafe for a hospitalized patient.

Another example is the need for many equine therapy programs to have mid age range horses with no stumbling in their gait. In Spirit Horse II, there are few programs that exist in our work that do not find a stumbley horse to be an advantage for several reasons. We therefore often accept therapeutic horses from other programs when they begin to falter, or are felt to be too unsteady for their programs. We have a 39 year old Arabian quarter mile racing horse that was out to stud for 12 years before he was sold down. We rescued him and he is one of our most in demand horses. He no longer is expected to have riders, but he is a trainer for wrapping legs, putting on performance or health care boots, and other stall or performance care projects. He loves the attention, the students love that he is extremely safe for them. Most of our students, by the time they reach higher levels of performance grooming are deeply in love with this horse, and really glad of a chance to learn show standard braiding with him, rather than on a young show horse.

Our certifications are made by our Directing Trainer, our veterinarian, our physical therapists, and psychologists together. Each animal has a file that lists his or her latest certification review. The tag for each animal contains a notation of exactly what areas that animal is certified for. We also use animals that are in process of gaining a level of competence and experience to be certified, their tags are noted as "in training". Many of our animals are owned by trainers, staff, volunteers and community members. None of our animals is ever sold down. In the event that the vet recommends euthanasia, our animals are humanely put down. We feel death is part of life, and the responsible care of animals includes the reality that in captivity animals often outlive their own health. We feel this is an educational part of our program, as well as part of our responsibility model in animal care and training.

Levels of competency are:

1. Behavior. Our team assesses our animals prior to accepting them into the program and periodically during the year, or if an incident or concern is raised by a rider, staff, volunteer, or therapists. We expect our animals to behave in a safe and non-aggressive manner towards humans and other animals. Our human therapists and assistants are all required to be certified in our own program levels as described in our certification material.

2. Health. Our team and our vet assesses our animals twice a year. Each animal is assessed each day by staff and therapists. The Directing Trainer may be asked to make a

decision about soundness for the day's activities. The vet techs and vet are the final opinion as to whether an animal is fit for the day's activity. Any animal not sound will be referred to the vet for care until released back to work. All humans must have an annual check up from their personal physician for doing the level of work they are doing in Spirit Horse II programs.

3. Training. Our animals are utilized for a variety of programs. Each animal has a file that contains the areas that animal is certified for or is in training for. All animals are rigorously trained to accept wheelchairs, canes, crutches, and personal hygiene products attached to the riders. Animals in training may have issues, this is covered in our orientation with our riders and staff. We feel it is important for our riders to be aware that while our goal is to educate animal owners to have their animals safe around disabled persons, it is not reality, and the disabled persons need to be aware of animals that are not as well trained as ours and be safe. Therefore, we train our animals on site and with real riders, not just with our own staff using similar healthcare equipment and items.

4. Care. Our animals are expected to be cared for by many classes and private riders each day. Our staff uses files and office day boards to make sure each animal is bathed regularly, is fed appropriately and has seen the shoer and other animal care experts as necessary. A big part of our program is to have the participants take care of the animals, therefore most animals are cared for in a daily routine several times each day. Each animal has its own living area as the Directing Trainer and vet certify. Our animals are not loaned or rented out.

5. Safety. Both animals and humans are expected to use safety gear as suggested by the activity. Adults "may" sign a waiver and refuse to wear safety riding helmets only for exhibitions. At all other times even adult riders

must wear regulation safety helmets. All riders are given an orientation in horse, and other animal safety and will be written up and may be excused from the program if they fail to follow safety regulations. ALL staff and volunteers are trained to address safety issues, and if necessary to contact the day Director, or the Spirit Horse II Director to handle issues. Safety stirrups are of choice. All performance level riders are to use the standard for the sport. Which often does not include safety stirrups. ALL staff are to realize that the ONLY riders to utilize safety belts, are those who work in a small round corral, with at least four horse handlers, a physical therapist and a specifically seat belt safety trained horse. Spirit Horse II considers being attached in any way to a horse to be inherently life threatening and is not to be done except as described above for severely physically disabled riders. The use of a safety belt is only with the presence of the physical therapist, and upon written prescription of the attending physician to the rider. The use of a safety belt is only with the written permission of both parents, or legal guardians.

6. The safety rules are to be posted and in at least two languages at all sites. ALL riders with different language needs are to be given the safety orientation in their own language, and to sign waivers in their own language. Spirit Horse II prefers that all riding members learn commands, and horse safety cues in English. In an emergency, the person needing to be heard may not know any other language. When riding on trails, in shows, and in rental stables, the only language may be English. Spirit Horse II feels it is important to know all safety cues in English.

7. There is NO horseplay allowed. While we encourage fun, and to experience joy with animals and while riding, no horseplay is allowed. The Spirit Horse II philosophy is that these ALL are wild animals. No matter how reliable, an

animal, or even a human can reach a breaking point. It is extremely important to have all participants, whether staff, volunteers, riders or guests to be in compliance. They will get one warning, then be asked to leave the premises. This includes, but it not limited to unsafe horse activities, bullying, name calling, gossip, cliques, and practical jokes. We consider all of these negative behaviors.

8. NO smoking around horses, riders, guests or barns. When the stable and barns are closed, the staff and volunteers "may" designate one safe smoking area, however, Spirit Horse II is a non-smoking environment during work hours and in the stables and hay barns. Riders need to respect that the stables and barns are used for literacy and high risk youth programs. No smoking is part of the health education program for all of our programs and needs to be respected.

9. 9. Recycling and no littering are both taught and upheld. Part of the Spirit Horse II program is to teach respect for the earth and the personal responsibility of each human to take part in not polluting, and not littering our earth, oceans, and other environmental resources.

10. NO FOOD is allowed to be brought on the site. Snacks, and meals are served as part of the nutrition programs, many foods are deadly to the animals and must be kept out of our environment. Carrots, apples, mints, and other horse snacks, approved dog and other small animal treats are available from staff. NO ANIMALS are to be fed without asking a staff person. Horses and dogs often eat food wrappers. This can be deadly. The small cellophane straw wrappers from juice boxes are often eaten, and become glued to the intestines of horses. Dogs and other therapy animals. They cause serious infections and death. DO NOT bring any food or drinks to the sites.

11. Shots. Our animals and handlers are all vaccinated regularly. Tetanus is the most common vaccine needed

by visitors to stables. Staph infections, in the cleanest of stables is a constant threat WASH YOUR HANDS. Food staff wears gloves for preparation and serving of food. Stables that have reptiles have a threat of salmonella as well. WASH YOUR HANDS after any contact with the reptiles, ducks, or chickens.

12. ILLNESS. Please do NOT come to Spirit Horse II ill. Many of our riders are disabled and their health compromised. They do not need your cold, sore throat, or flu. If you have taken antibiotics for 48 hours, and your doctor feels you may safely return to the program, you may, but are not required to take class, work or volunteer when ill. Our riders health is too important to compromise. Horses also are very subject to illness. Do not bring outside horses, tack or items to our stable areas without permission and proper disinfecting procedures being taken. WASH YOUR HANDS when you arrive to make sure you do not spread something from your own pets to our working partners.

EXTENDED PROGRAMS

Spirit Horse II has many ongoing expanded programs which include high risk Boy Scouts of America Venture Crew programs, juvenile probation and regional center vendors who bring their clients to the programs. The programs for children of veterans, and active duty service personnel, as well as children of first responders are included in the veteran's service project.

Many of our programs include performance and exhibition teams and private riding programs for riders who have advanced beyond treatment programs.

Our staff and volunteers enjoy the use of many of our program facilities at all times as long as they do not interfere with ongoing treatment classes. Spirit Horse II gives a series of exhibition programs in partnership with local parks and schools to give the opportunity of our programs to children, teens and adults who may never have any other chance to experience a real working horse environment. We trailer horses to events in partnership with juvenile probation, parks, and local police and sheriff events. We have our own Spirit Horse II safety regulations for this type of event. ALL staff and volunteers have to complete a special training program and be certified before being allowed to attend a trailered out event.

Spirit Horse II encourages our riders, staff and volunteers to do exhibit and performance riding in shows, parades, and other events. Each of these events must be approved by the Training Director in writing prior to being announced publicly, if the name National Homes for Heroes/Spirit Horse II is used to promote the event.

Spirit Horse II encourages media coverage and filming. Each of our riders is notified and signs a waiver that encompasses the most open relationship with media and the entertainment industry. Any problems are to be reported immediately to the Training Director in writing.

INCIDENT REPORTING-Youth Protection Act

Spirit Horse II utilizes a system of Government Mandated and Trained Youth Protection and protection of the disabled that is supported by our systems rules.

NUMBER ONE: BUDDY system. When a person signs in to Spirit Horse II, they must be signed in with a buddy. At no time are the two buddies to lose sight of each other!

NUMBER TWO: Log book. If there is a complaint or incident, it MUST be reported in writing to the stable day staff in writing in the log book. Orientation includes the warning that if an incident is not reported within 24 hours and the appropriate incident report filed, it did not happen! There are no exceptions.

We train ALL of our membership that when someone says "don't tell", you have to "tell". If no one else, speak directly to the Training Director.

NUMBER THREE: The incident report includes all relevant information. Each site director is responsible within 48 hours of a log in to put the incident in the computerized log book for Spirit Horse II and to submit a copy of the incident report electronically. Hard copy is to be kept on site for ONE YEAR. All hard copy is sent after one year to the Training Director, then to the lawyers for safe keeping for twenty-five (25) years.

If any person, complainant, staff or Training Director feels the complaint involves child abuse, it must be reported to the police within one hour of notification of the log keeper. The "Buddy" statement is required on the incident report and must be taken immediately. ALL other witnesses or potential witness must be identified on the incident report. When parents are calling to report an incident they are expected to go over the entire incident report with the complainant and the Buddy prior to filing. Mandatory mediation and /or dispute resolution are to be instituted immediately upon request by the Training Director. ALL records must be kept for one year with the incident report, and filed electronically with Spirit Horse II as they are filed on site.

The Training Director will have all of these files kept in hard copy for twenty-five years, by a Law Firm on retainer for this purpose only.

Horses, animals and youth are a prescription for injuries. Spirit Horse II has a prescribed regulatory method to deal with injuries.

1. CALL 911 IF NECESSARY THEN, CALL THE PARENTS if they are not present. FIND THE TRAINING DIRECTOR.
2. Fill in the log, fill out the incident report. Take pictures if possible. GET THE BUDDY STATEMENT.
3. ALL adults are also required to be within sight of another certified adult at all times. ANY problems may be put in the log and handled by the Training Director or the site Director and referenced to the Training Director.
4. ALL adults are required to have live scan fingerprints done periodically for staff, or volunteers at any Spirit Horse II site. Parents are encouraged to accompany their children to all classes and events. Grandparents, paid parenting staff are encouraged to accompany children. ALL visitors and rider family members MUST be logged in and given a day-pass that limits areas they are to be allowed. Parents, Grandparents, and other guests are to stay within eyesight of the rider they are visiting. This is to make sure no one's guests are wandering around treatment and youth areas without staff supervision.

For safety: Spirit Horse II utilizes one type of handicapped accessible restroom for riders and guests. Staff and volunteers have their own restrooms. ONE person in the restroom at a time, ONE buddy waiting outside for safety. ADULTS are requested not to linger near the restrooms, and to be accompanied by their assigned staff or buddy for their own safety as well as that of the riders. False abuse claims are damaging to adults: Spirit Horse II asks all adults to adhere to the rules to minimize risk to our juveniles, and disabled persons, and to minimize risk of false claims against adults.

Some types of emergency:

LOOSE HORSE.

A loose horse in a highly populated stable area is very dangerous. Even a usually calm horse may get frightened and trample someone if too many people try to catch the horse, or are just in the way.

If you hear someone yell "loose horse" move close to a building, or tree, or vehicle. Stand still, and if the horse approaches, wave your arms to wave the animal away. Do NOT yell, or scare the horse further. Let horse staff retrieve the animal ONLY. If you, or someone near you is in a wheelchair, or on crutches, get as close as possible to a very large object, tree, vehicle, or inside until the horse is caught. Please help wheelchair and other persons who need help. Safety is the utmost importance.

FALLEN RIDER

When a rider falls, stand still. If you are on horseback, stop the horse and stand still. Let the staff take care of the emergency. If you are asked to dismount and return your animal to the barn early, do it. The safety of the person who has fallen is more important than if your class was cut short.

LISTEN TO THE STAFF. The staff will direct everyone safely. Please listen and do as you are asked.

Do NOT chase the rider's horse. Let staff take care of recapturing the horse and calming the situation down.

IN THE ARENA OR ROUND CORRAL DO NOT tie horses to the fences. EVER.

LOOK to see if another horse is in the arena, or round corral before opening the gate.

Follow directions of staff around the horses when working in the arena and/or round corrals.

WASHING HORSES

Spirit Horse II has allowed two philosophies. The first is to NEVER tie a horse while grooming and washing. Either a second person holds the horse, or the rider is certified to handle a horse alone and takes care of both holding the horse and washing it or grooming it. Many of our horses are groomed prior to riding in their own stalls and are NOT tied up. Follow the directions of staff.

The second philosophy is people who believe in cross tying. Follow the directions and learn safety around cross tied horses. While Spirit Horse II does not believe in this practice, many of our horses are privately owned. Their owners have used cross tying and are not comfortable with natural horsemanship grooming techniques. Therefore, we allow this exception to our rule.

SHOERS

When the shoers are working, EVERONE is to pay attention to the requests of the shoer. Some horses are very stressed by shoeing and need quiet and to be left alone. Other horses like a human handler to hold them, others are tied to a post and fine. Listen to the shoers. They are hired for their expertise and know when a horse is not feeling well and behaving poorly. It is not up to riders or guests to say "but I know this horse, he loves me". Listen and be safe, the shoers need to be safe, and the horses need to be safe.

VETS

When the vets are tending horses, everyone must listen to the vet and vet techs and do as they ask. These are professionals who need to be safe around huge, injured or ill animals. Spirit Horse II wants riders, guests and volunteers to experience all aspects of horse care, however, when the vet or vet tech asks for people to leave the scene. Do so at once. Quietly.

OTHER ANIMALS in the programs.

Many volunteers and staff bring their own dogs and other pets to share with the riders and their families. The animals are in training, or certified animal assisted therapy course completion animals. PLEASE treat all animals with respect and care. It can be overwhelming for an animal to be rushed by several persons. Think about how you would feel, and be respectful of the animals. Mother animals are often vicious in protecting their young. ASK before handling any baby animals, chickens, ducks, or going near mares with foals.

Mares who are about to foal often are guided by their instinct to be alone, they may bite or kick, when usually they are gentle and safe horses. Do not bother the mares, ASK staff for permission before approaching them.

FOAL imprinting and colt development

Spirit Horse II is a Native American Natural Horsemanship practicing program. We believe that horses do not need to be hit, kicked, or abused into obeying. We also have trainers who have trained with vets and trainers who practice foal imprinting and colt development. In the first hours of a young horse's life the trainers and vet techs will work with the animal to imprint many later working skill lessons on the young horse. In colt development, similar exercises are done to prepare the young horse for a seamless and easy transition to a rideable horse. Please do not interfere in these sessions.

Spirit Horse II
Animal Assisted Therapy-Certification of Therapy Animals

Elizabeth Wiley, MA, JD Trainer/Director

Spirit Horse II-therapuetic modality descriptions

Equine Assisted Literacy Program

Spirit Horse II has credentialed special education teachers who have created their own literacy programs that include, but are not limited to reading, writing and learning about horses. The programs are designed with the IEP or approval of the treating doctor (if any) to facilitate a joy of learning and increase age and grade level skills.

Public school programs that promote reading are part of our free community projects that each Spirit Horse II site will participate in locally, and Spirit Horse II will participate in nationally and internationally to promote literacy.

Freeworldu.org is utilized by Spirit Horse II as a free mentoring program.

Family literacy programs are Spirit Horse II programs that encourage families to learn old family stories, to find out facts and history of the family and to share these stories in our international literacy project.

Physical Therapy-Equine assisted physical therapy programs are in two programs.

The Equine assisted therapy program is accomplished with the prescription of a doctor or psychologist. Many of the students in this program are accompanied by their county approved vendors from regional treatment centers. The staff is expected to accompany and stay with the riders at all times and to fill out the one sheet observation page to be returned to the prescribing doctor. Spirit Horse II does not keep any records, it is the responsibility of the staff and prescribing physician.

The Equine Therapy program also requires a prescribing physician or psychiatrist, if necessary. Spirit Horse II has licensed and certified equine therapists who work at the sites. Spirit Horse II Equine Therapists fill out a one page, numbered observation sheet for each class and mail it to the prescribing physician or psychiatrist. THESE records are kept electronically for ONE WEEK only in case of loss in the mail.

Emotional Equine Assisted Therapy

Programs for high risk youth and children of vets and active duty service personnel, as well as Mommy and Me Ride, and Daddy and Me Ride programs are non –specific and have staff that is certified to work in our own unique Spirit Horse II programs. These all were developed and are overseen by our own psychologists and behavioral specialists.

These programs are offered free to community projects such as Juvenile Probation, Housing, schools, Head Start, religious and Scouting programs.

These programs include: Kids Anonymous (a program for teens in divorce, death or other stressful situations) and Kids

Jr (a program for children in divorce, death or other stressful situations), 12 Steps Home (for vets and their families) and 12 Steps Home from Betrayal by Brothers at Arms (for vets who have been sexually assaulted in combat zones). These are quasi twelve step programs developed by the kids, and the vets themselves. Spirit Horse II is in the process of finding out how, or if, they can become real 12 step programs. As in all 12 step programs peer support, rather than professionals is the rule. While adult supervisors or staff are present for the children and teen programs, they are there for safety, not to interfere in the process. We called AA and asked how to become real 12 Step programs, they said to email the programs. We did. We have never heard yay or nay, so still are considering ourselves quasi-12 Step.

Meditation, yoga, stress reduction, anger management, mediation programs

Programs to help our staff, riders, families and guests improve their lives are offered on a continuous basis. Most of these programs are free of charge and open to the public if the space is available.

Spirit Horse II refers all drug, alcohol and other addicts to outside programs and treatment.

Gardening and Green programs

Plants, animals and the outdoors are a part of the therapeutic environment at Spirit Horse. Grooming, care of tack and stables and kennels and other animal areas is part of the program. Spirit Horse II does not allow anyone to come to a program without full participation in all areas of animal care, and group programs where required by Spirit Horse II.

Art, Drama, Music programs

Art in many forms, Drama, Music and Dance are all a part of programs offered at Spirit Horse II.

Field Trips and family inclusive events

From work done with the Y WINGS programs in the wake of Desert Storm, Spirit Horse II started a program of field trips and family inclusive events, such as trips to rodeos, horse shows, parades, and performances or school programs for other members to show support. Spirit Horse II has a credentialed teacher to schedule field trips. Fundraising is utilized to help reduce the cost and scholarships to families as needed are a goal of each event or field trip. We use school bus service local to each Spirit Horse II site for transportation. Children who do not have a family adult to accompany them are encouraged to be included as part of another family approved by their parents or guardians. Spirit Horse II is a diversity supporting program and refrains from calling a family a "mom and dad and kids". Many children in high risk programs have parents in service, or prison, or dead. Spirit Horse II uses our education programs and events to help children include others, rather than exclude or identify "otherness" as a negative for children already deeply stressed by their realities.

Spirit Horse II has specific events for children of terminally ill parents or siblings. These were created by AIDS Project Pasadena many years ago, and Spirit Horse II feels this type of event gives a day of support to hurting children. Each child is paired with two pre-approved adult family members, friends, or staff and volunteers to have a complete day, even in a group, just for them.

Spirit Horse II has an open door ride free policy for terminally ill patients and their families to come and observe and participate as much as possible in any of our classes and events.

From Cowboy life-skill classes to stressed executives who volunteer and feed carrots and groom horses a few hours a month, Spirit Horse II shares a moment of respite from a world that is outside the gates. As our vet told us "when a horse comes here, they have it made", we hope this is true for our staff, riders, and volunteers and guests at all times.

We strive for that to be our service.

FORMS-SPIRIT HORSE II

Horse Registration Form

Name of horse: Nickname (if one):
Date horse came to Spirit Horse: Stall number:
Owned by:
Address and phone number for owner:
Preferred vet: or signature of owner to use our own
vets _____ date _____
Age of horse
Mare/Colt/Stallion/Gelding
History of horse

Last known shots, worming, known medical needs, special feed needs, special shoeing needs

Please attach horse worming and vaccination table and put horse on next stable schedule for worming and vaccinations.

BE specific, what will owner be doing with horse, and what days will owner want to use horse so it will be unavailable for class work. Remind owners to let us know in advance of special events, or performances when horse will be out of Spirit Horse II.

Spirit Horse IIICarousel
Horse Workbook

Date	Vaccinations	Worming	Shoer	Bathed (li,twholo month in column)

OTHER BOOKS BY AUTHOR

Reassessing and Restructuring Public Agencies: What to do to save our Country

Carousel Horse: a teaching inclusive book about equine therapy

Spirit Horse II: Equine therapy manuals and workbooks

Could This Be Magic: a VERY short book about the time I spent with VAN HALEN

Dollars in the Streets-Lydia Caceres Edited by Author about first woman horse trainer at Belmont Park

Addicted to Dick: a healing book quasi Twelve Step for women with addiction to mean men

Addicted to Dick-2018 Edition Self help and training manual for women who allow men to torture, molest and kill their children

BOOKS TO BE RELEASED:

America CAN live happily ever after: first in series of Americans resolving all the issues

America CAN live happily ever after 2: Second in series of HOW to go out and BE equal, and to part of the OF the, BY the and FOR the People our Constitution guarantees us. If the school is not teaching your children, go down and read, do math, join a science project, do lunchtime Scouting for the kids, go sit in the hallways with your smart phone and take lovely action video for the parents of kids who do not behave. More. Many suggestions from parents, and how to fundraise.

Carousel Two: Equine therapy for veterans

Still Spinning: Equine therapy for women veterans

Legal Ethics: An Oxymoron???

Friend Bird: A children's book about loneliness and how to conquer it (adults will love it too)

Kids Anonymous and Kids Jr. quasi twelve step books for and by youth and teens

12 Steps Back from Betrayal from Brothers at Arms and 12 Steps Home two quasi twelve step books and work books

created by author and veterans, and author's Father for Native American and other veterans

BIG LIZ: The Leader of the Gang Racial Tension and Gang Abatement work by author

PLEASE join the tee shirt contests by checking the web sites on the books and contacting the link provided. WE love children, teens and adults helping us to give our classes free, and spread the word of our work. ALL of our work is done through education projects by our high risk youth, veterans and first responders page NATIONAL HOMES FOR HEROES/SPIRIT HORSE II. We are just getting back to full work due to cancer of the two Directors and vehicle accidents and our stable burning down in a forest fire a couple of years ago. We promise to get more organized as we move along. 2019is our first year of taking nominations and awarding a Keiry Equine Therapy Award. We will also need poster and tee shirt designs for that. See Carousel Horse and Spirit Horse II links to nominate a program. God bless us, as Tiny Tim said, Everyone.

Printed in the United States
By Bookmasters